STAR

TRICKS:

BACKSTORIES

©2011

David A Shaffer

Author Photo
© 2009 M. P. Ramos

ISBN-13:
978-1456311841

ISBN-10:
1456311840

Privately Published by David A Shaffer

FOREWORD

My name is Kirk James. If you purchased this book to catch up on my adventures, I fear you will be disappointed. If you have been reading my previous collections of journals, published as Star Tricks, More Star Tricks, Star Tricks Three, and Star Tricks Four, you will know that there are many people in my life who are very important to me.

While I was visiting Stewardess Marana of the Enterprisian Star Cluster as related in Star Tricks Four, she gave me a file left to her by the late Queen Colata. This amounted to some fifteen pages and I wanted to share it with my loyal readers but could find no place for it in that volume. Of course, it is much too small to publish separately. After some thought, I decided to ask several of my friends to write autobiographies to be compiled with Colata's missive into a volume suitable to stand alone with my other published works.

Once I get this volume 'in the works', I'll return to my usual job of keeping you up to date on my life.

Kirk M. James

Fleet Admiral, United Federation of Planets

CHAPTER I: Colata

My name is Colata. As I write this, I am queen of the sixteen planet monarchy known as Enterprisia. Of course, I was not always queen and the monarchy was not always known as Enterprisia. As I write this, I am preparing for the birth of my son. From the way my body feels, I suspect that I will not survive this birth and I wish to tell my story for all to read. The doctors attempt to reassure me that nothing is wrong but I am convinced that I will not survive this birth.

But even though I suspect that the end of my life is near, I am extremely happy. How could I not be? Despite my poor beginnings, I have known great joy; I now live in the finest luxury. And I am in love with the finest man in this or any galaxy. While it is true that I do not see him often, those few visits more than make up for the absences and I have Marana for comfort while my darling must be away. I have never mustered the courage to tell him how I feel but surely he knows.

To properly tell the story, I should begin with some history. My home world was originally

7

known as Roatta. Many generations ago, our people discovered energy-gathering fields and star travel. With these, we colonized fifteen nearby planets, forming a sixteen planet kingdom, ruled from Roatta. This, while difficult to administer, was a stable and generally happy political entity until about three generations before my birth. At about that time, an unscrupulous man plotted with some other political ingrates and they managed to assassinate the popular king. This usurper managed to seize control of the kingdom by brute force and declared himself Emperor.

Realizing that the existing Royal Family would be a threat to his crown, the new Emperor declared them to be outlaws and sentenced any who were captured to be held as slaves. This, of course, drove all of the Royal Family into hiding using disguises and assumed names. Slaves proved to be so popular with the ruling class that any 'inconvenient person' risked becoming a slave.

My mother, Viana, grew up free as a simple country girl called Velma. She knew from early girlhood that she was truly a Princess but she must keep that secret. However, it was her solemn duty to bear an heir to the throne in the event that the Emperor could someday be overthrown. She swore to uphold the duty but was hampered by the lack of contact with other Royal Family members. In an attempt to be true to her destiny, my mother kept herself pure, waiting for a Royal Family member.

She finally came in contact with an organized resistance movement. The leader of the local cell was a fiery young man named

Multa. Viana and Multa soon fell in love but she had promised her mother and others so she waited.

With Multa's grudging assistance, Viana contacted the secret Society of Heralds and met a gardener for one of the Emperor's cronies who was known as Pembra. The gardener was actually Arch Duke Pembroke and in direct line of succession to the throne. He was a very old man and she did not find him attractive but she felt it was her duty to bear a child by him. It took repeated attempts over a long period of time before she was certain she was with child. Pembra was sorry to see it end but Viana was ecstatic.

Now Viana was free to spend time with Multa and they got to know each other well.

Multa's parents had both been leaders in the resistance but had been killed when their cell was betrayed to Imperial forces. His sister, Sanda, had been taken as a slave. Multa had sworn to free his sister and avenge his parents but being an uncommonly wise young man, he knew he must bide his time.

I was born and spent my first twelve years living as the daughter of a free seamstress. My mother told me of my true heritage and impressed on me the importance of secrecy.

Shortly after my twelfth birthday, Mother took me to a meeting of Multa's underground cell. She would have preferred to keep me away for safety reasons but she was loath to leave me unprotected.

9

Imperial forces raided the cell meeting. We never learned how we were betrayed but such things happened often. Multa and a few of his assistants managed to fight their way free but Mother and I were captured. Many others were killed or captured.

So Mother and I became slaves in the home of a wealthy Emperor supporter. My duties were to work in the kitchen and, unfortunately, the men found me attractive so I was forced often to serve their pleasure. One day, after an especially brutal night with a guest of the master, I was comforted by one of the other female slaves. I found this much more pleasant than contact with men and after that, I sought the comfort of women.

Shortly before my eighteenth birthday, a new Emperor ascended the throne. This one's name was Klug and if anything, he was worse than the ones before him. One of his first acts was to change the name of our planet from Roatta to Klug. I swore that if I ever claimed my proper throne, one of my first acts would be to fix that.

As slaves, we were not allowed much access to news of the worlds outside but occasional items of information would reach us. Multa had become a General of the Rebel Forces and they were becoming a serious threat to the Emperor's troops. The Emperor was offering huge rewards for information leading to Multa's death or arrest. Multa's sister, Sanda, was not kept in the same house as we so we never met her or knew of her fate.

Amazingly, our Royal status was never revealed during our long captivity. Mother was

10

simply Velma and I was Colata, the kitchen slave and plaything. During this interminable ordeal, I became pregnant several times but that was corrected by the master's physician. This was not any kindness on the master's part; he merely didn't want me incapacitated. The master himself enjoyed my services occasionally when he had no guests to entertain. I can't say that I enjoyed these duties but I did sleep in a better bed and usually ate much better food.

In my seventeenth year, our master moved us all to his new home on the planet Kinsala. The new house was larger and more comfortable but as slaves, our duties were only increased because the house was larger.

Most of my master's guests were reasonably kind and gentle with me. I tried to encourage this treatment by being extra pleasing to them. When a guest became rough or violent, I had no opportunity to refuse him favors but I was not so willing. When I was injured, my master would allow me medical treatment and time to recover.

One of the few privileges I enjoyed as my master's plaything was access to his extensive library. My kitchen and other duties left little time for reading but I have always been hungry for knowledge and my master's library stocked a vast collection of classic literature. Mother had seen to it that I learned to read at an early age so I was able to educate myself very well.

In this manner, I spent my adolescence and young womanhood. It certainly was not a typical education but I learned a lot.

Then, on my twenty-fifth birthday, an event changed the world for Mother and me.

It all began with an attack on the house by rebel troops. Master only had a few bodyguards and they had little chance against heavily armed and seasoned troops. The fighting only lasted for a few minutes but we were all terrified. Even though this was the only home we had known for many years, we all secretly hoped that the rebels would be victorious.

Our wishes came true. The leader of the Rebel troops, Lieutenant Kawa, assigned one of his squad leaders, Sergeant Colena, to lead all of the freed slaves back to the ship after ascertaining that Mother and I were in the group.

We were treated with special respect and deference but we had truly forgotten our Royal blood after all these years.

Once we arrived at the ship, Mother and I were given the best stateroom available and people began to treat us as royalty. This confused and upset us after being slaves for so long. A couple of the female crew members gave us dresses and after we were bathed, we were attired in the finest clothing either of us had ever worn. After this, we were treated to the most excellent food the ship had to offer.

Somehow, the rebels had learned of our existence and location. General Multa felt that the people would want me to lead them once the rebels overthrew the evil Emperor so he set about setting Mother and me free.

But first, we needed to reach safety.

The ship carrying us to the rebel stronghold was called the *Defiant* and she was under the command of Captain Krill.

"Thank you so much, Captain. You and the ground troops have certainly saved us."

"Don't thank us yet, Your Highness. We're being pursued by an Imperial Cruiser that is both bigger and better armed than we are. I'm calling for help but it isn't certain that help can reach us in time."

"Can we run faster?"

"Velocity should be about equal but we have no place to go. With that Cruiser following us, we can't go to our base without revealing its location. And he's not likely to give up. And no doubt he's calling for help too."

"What will you do?"

"All I can think of is to surprise him by turning suddenly to fight. With luck, we might be able to penetrate his screens and cripple him."

But Captain Krill's desperate gamble failed. It was the *Defiant* that found herself crippled and losing atmosphere.

Then, like a miracle foretold in a prophecy, another ship appeared on the viewer.

"Attacking ship, this is Captain Kirk James, commanding the *USS Enterprise*. Stop your attack immediately or be destroyed."

"Who are you and why is this your business?"

"We are representatives of the United Federation of Planets. We will tolerate no more of this violence. Stop immediately."

"And if we choose to fight?"

"You will be destroyed,"

Thus, the only man I could ever love made his dramatic entrance into my life.

The *Enterprise* proved to be much more than the Imperial Cruiser could handle. After sending the Emperor's minions home in disgrace, Captain James helped the *Defiant* to our intended destination.

When we landed, Mother and I were treated as Royal persons and I began to worry that I was not prepared to act as a queen. While I had educated myself as well as possible, I knew nothing of laws or government. If I actually found myself in command of sixteen planets, many lives would depend on my every word and action. I just didn't feel ready for that. The ever-wise Captain James told of a system on his home world where the monarch was a mostly ceremonial position while the actual lawmaking was done by an elected parliament. General Multa agreed that the system sounded ideal for us and said he would do all he could do to implement such a system.

That was when I fell hopelessly in love with Captain Kirk James. Not only was he handsome and brave, he was wise and caring. He already had a wife but I learned that she was willing to share him and did so frequently.

Over the next few months, Captain James and the other Federation ships assisted the rebel forces in overcoming Klug's Empire. Multa was a magnificent leader but even he admitted that he would have gone down to defeat without Federation intervention.

Captain James was always modest about his part in this. Many of the most brilliant ideas were his but he refused to take credit, always giving someone else the praise that was his due.

When I reluctantly ascended the throne, the only enticement that actually drove me was the opportunity to recognize Captain James for the true hero he was to our entire commonwealth. Of course, I found it necessary to praise the other heroes at the same time and all deserved it but Kirk was my true target. I insisted on kissing every starship captain just for the chance to kiss Captain James.

In keeping my promise to myself, I changed the name of our capital planet to Enterprisia in honor of my lover's ship and indeed, I changed the name of the entire commonwealth in his honor.

All too soon, Captain James and the other federation ships went about their business. Kirk had promised to visit and he did so twice over the next few months. He was, however, apparently oblivious of my feelings for him. Either that or he was exceedingly discreet.

General Multa had become a powerful peacetime leader, mostly because people trusted him and were accustomed to his strong leadership. When he proposed the elected parliament with a token monarchy and I strongly supported the idea, the people liked it too. Fortunately, we had always had elected governments at the planetary level with a Royal

Viceroy nominally in charge so the transition was not terribly difficult.

My transition from slave to queen was much more time-consuming. Late one sleepless night, I found myself desiring a snack and made my way to the kitchen where I found a kitchen assistant of about my age polishing silver.

"This silver looks very good but there is a much easier way to do it. Let me show you."

"But Your Highness, you'll ruin your hands."

"They were ruined many years ago anyway. Besides that, the Royal Manicurist needs work too."

So I sat up for hours helping her polish silver and chatting. I learned that her name was Mina and I finally convinced her to call me Colata, at least in private. She and her family had managed to remain free under the Emperors but they had by no means had an easy life. She was currently raising a small son on the salary she was earning working at the Palace. I discovered that this employment was one of the best she could hope to have; offering very good pay for relatively light effort.

"One of the best parts is that I can send my son to sleep with a trusted friend while I work. By the time he is ready to rise, I have finished work."

"But when do you sleep?"

"I can nap occasionally during the day while Milo plays."

"Are there others here doing the same thing?"

16

"I know of several women who have small children and prefer to work nights so they can be there for the children in the daytime."

"That cannot be healthy for the mothers or the children. Let me see if I can arrange a child care center for Palace employees. I believe that the service should be provided free of charge so that all loyal and hard-working employees can get some sleep and live more normal lives. This will also provide jobs for those caring for the children."

"I can't believe that our queen takes an interest in such small matters."

"It really isn't such a small matter to me. I recently learned that one of my duties is to bear an heir to the throne. I suppose I knew that but had never thought of it. My long years as a slave left me with a loathing for most men. The few suitable Royal Family members are either much too old, much too young, or, frankly, turn my stomach. As another woman, what do you advise?"

"What does your heart tell you?"

"There is only one man I want but he bears no Royal Blood. Furthermore, while he has always been noble and caring, he has never shown any romantic interest in me. I have no way of knowing if he is uninterested or merely discreet."

"Can the Royal Blood obstacle be overcome?"

"I suppose I could grant him a title. Some people might object but he was a mighty hero of the revolution so there should be strong support."

"Are you speaking of that dreamy Captain James?"

"Indeed I am."

"I don't blame you a bit. If I thought I had a chance, I'd trip him and beat him to the ground."

This set off a giggling match.

"So I'm not the only one who feels that way."

"Well, he's not only good-looking, he saved sixteen planets and proved incredibly wise and brave doing so."

"I had to kiss a lot of ugly starship captains just to get to him."

"I think I'd make that sacrifice."

More giggling.

"So what will you do next?"

"As you know, I've taken a female Consort. I love Marana dearly but she can't help me provide an heir. We've talked and she agrees that Captain James would be ideal if the obstacles can be overcome. I think she'd like a chance with him too. I intend to invite Kirk, Captain James, here on some pretense and see if I can seduce him."

"My lady, if I can be of any assistance, you only need call." Wide grin.

I wanted to discuss my scheme with Mother but was forced to wait three days because she and General Multa had taken an 'extended trip' together. I didn't begrudge them this time together, knowing of their interrupted past. After they returned, I sought out Mother at the first opportunity.

"So what do you think of Kirk as Father to the Heir to the Throne?"

"If we can find a way to make him acceptable to the general populace, I believe he has every other quality necessary. But are you certain he'll be willing?"

"That remains to be seen. But remember, I spent many years learning to manipulate men. That training just has to have some use."

"I suspect that Kirk may be difficult to manipulate. Perhaps a better approach would be to tell him the absolute truth and allow him to decide for himself."

"You may be right. I'll do it that way. Now, there's the matter of his title."

"Well, the planet Strombala has not had a Duke since Stoor died heirless."

"But that isn't a very desirable planet. Very few people live there or care to."

"Kirk wouldn't need to live there or even visit. You grant him the title of Duke of Strombala and that makes him of Royal Blood. The fact that he's never even seen the planet is immaterial."

"Do you think the people will accept this?"

"The people love you and they love Kirk. I'm sure they'll want to see the two of you produce a Royal Heir together. They seem fascinated by the 'doings' of the Royal Family anyway and as long as you do things properly, you can get away with almost anything."

"I also wonder if that beautiful wife, Free, will allow this."

"When I spoke to her, she told me that both of them enjoy the company of others on a regular basis. Kirk plays exclusively with females but Free likes males and females."

"So perhaps Marana can entertain Free while I monopolize Kirk. She's mentioned several times how attractive she thought Free is."

"By the way, Multa told me that Kirk is now an Admiral of the Federation Fleet."

"I can't think of anyone who deserves it more."

"Well, why not call him and see if you can get him here?"

"Now I'm nervous."

"Queens don't get nervous; they pay somebody else to be nervous for them."

We both giggled.

****

"Admiral James, can we talk privately?"

"I can transfer this call to my office but if this can wait, we'll be on your planet in less than two days and we can talk in person."

"In person will be much better. Please, when you get here, I will leave word for you to be brought directly to me. Your wife, Free, is invited too. This is of a more personal than official nature but I need you badly."

"We will not delay."

"Thank you, Sir."

Well, he would be here soon. I just hoped I could convince him.

When they arrived, a Household Page showed them to my apartments.

"I'm glad you could come so quickly. You were always so kind and wise. You solved problems for me that no one else could begin to solve. Now I have another I hope you can solve."

"If there is anything I can do, I will be happy to try."

"As you know, I spent a major portion of my life as a kitchen slave. Only your timely intervention placed me on this throne. I did not have the benefit of the training and education that a queen in training should have. Your suggestion that we install a professional Prime Minister and elected Parliament has relieved me of many of the responsibilities of the throne. For that, I will be forever grateful. However, there is one duty that I cannot dodge and I am beginning to dread it. I hope you can help me find an answer."

"In what way can I help?"

"The custom is for the queen to bear an heir to the throne. When I was a kitchen slave, I was forced to serve the pleasure of men and now there are very few men who attract me. I turned to women for solace and mostly prefer women now. I have chosen a woman for a Royal Consort but I cannot have an heir with her. A female Consort is acceptable to the people but I must bear a child of a male of noble blood. There are very few males remaining after the Emperor finished with us and the few remaining are either ancient, children, or frankly, turn my stomach. Do you have any ideas that may help?"

"That does seem to be a difficult problem. You recently dubbed many knights. Are they considered to be of noble blood?"

"Unfortunately, no. Custom requires that a person must be at least a Duke to qualify."

21

I think he smelled a trap.

"If only you were single and of noble blood." I started easing the trap closed.

"Huh?"

"You are one of the very few males that has truly attracted me in all this time. Your gentle humor and wisdom, your bravery and honor, and your general attractiveness would make you the perfect father for the child I must have."

"But Kirk was recently proclaimed a Duke by the planet of Felana and I am not at all a jealous wife." Free spoke up. "I'll happily loan him to you."

"You would?" This would save me from naming Kirk the Duke of a laughingly useless planet.

"Of course. Would your consort consider keeping me company at the same time?"

"I'm sure she would." I smiled. "She saw a picture of you and remarked how much she admired you. Let me call her and we can all talk."

When Marana met Free in person, it was lust at first sight.

The next six weeks were like a dream come true for me. Kirk is not only brave, wise, and handsome, he's incredibly virile. After all these years trying to avoid men, I actually looked forward to bedtime. I was sorry to learn that I was pregnant and there was no need to continue.

Of course I had been examined frequently by the Royal Physician and before embarking on this plan, I had requested a specific examination pertaining to becoming

22

pregnant. The doctors had told me they could see no reason I should have any problem bearing children.

The first few months of my pregnancy went smoothly. I went about my official duties and the people made allowances for my reduced schedule as my pregnancy progressed.

But as I neared the end of the pregnancy, I started to have symptoms that concerned both my doctors and myself. I began bleeding in a way that certainly wasn't normal and at times the cramps were excruciating.

"It's far too early for the baby to survive on his own. If we remove the fetus, he'll die but if we allow the pregnancy to continue, your life is in danger."

"My son's life is more important than mine. I'll keep him as long as possible."

"Tests now show internal damage that was hidden before. This will be your only child. Those clumsy abortions you had when you were so young left so much damage that I'm amazed that you managed to carry a baby this long. The uterus is splitting badly this time and will definitely need to be removed after this child. One of the abortions also removed an ovary and now the other is damaged and will need removed. I'm sorry, Your Highness, but this child will be the only one you will bear."

"Then keep me alive long enough for him to have a chance at life. He is much more important than I. He's the future."

So I set about doing my best to survive long enough to give my baby a chance at life. Tests demonstrated that I was carrying a son and every indication was that he was entirely

23

normal and healthy. I merely needed to stay alive long enough for him to develop.

"Marana, there's a good chance that you'll be raising a son."

"Please don't talk that way, Colata."

"We must, Dearest. If I manage to survive, we can always pretend these words were never said but we should make plans."

"Okay, what do you want me to do?"

"Most important is the baby's name. I want to name him after his father but nearly everyone is naming their sons 'Kirk' so I want to name him 'James' after Kirk's other name. I understand that James is a popular given name on Earth."

"Okay, I'll see to that."

"Next, I want you to raise James as if he's your own child. Please take treatments so you can breast feed him. I believe that's the only proper way to feed an infant."

"I'll be proud and happy to do that."

"Now this next part might be more difficult. I want to name you Stewardess so you can hold the throne until James reaches the Age of Majority."

"Oh, my! That's a big job."

"You're smarter and better educated than I and you'll have Mother, General Multa, and any advisors you care to appoint. The people all love you and if I don't survive, you'll have their sympathy. Please do this for me."

"If that's what you really want. But I'm counting on you to live through this."

"I'll do my best."

But I already knew the birth would be my last act. Strangely, I'm not frightened or sad.

24

I feel that this birth is my whole reason for existing. Once James is born, I have no more real purpose. Marana will be his mother and will hold the throne until he can ascend it and be the king the commonwealth needs. I've packed a lot of living into a relatively short life and seen more than many people several times my age. And I've loved the finest man who ever existed.

I'll leave this on my computer for Marana to find. I hope she'll give it to Kirk. Maybe he can use it in one of his journals.

NOTE: Colata did indeed perish giving birth to James as described in Star Tricks Three. Marana is holding the throne as Stewardess until James reaches the age of majority at seventeen.

CHAPTER II: VREEK

Hello, I'm Vreek. I'm primarily writing this to residents of Earth so many of you know me as Governor of the Great State of New York.

As is no doubt self-evident, I am not a native of this great planet, Earth. Indeed, I hail from the Planet Graak but immigrated here in order to pursue my political career.

Admiral James has asked me to tell my story and I have a lot of story to tell. My people are extremely long-lived by Earth standards so I must try to give just the information that you may find necessary and interesting.

For those of you not familiar with my people, we strongly resemble Earth's common garden slug, except that we are many degrees of magnitude larger. If I stretch my body, I measure approximately twelve feet from the tip of my foremost part to the tip of my rearmost part. In my usual posture, the top of my head is about six feet above the ground. I possess two manipulating appendages or arms, one on each side of my body. These appendages resemble the arms of Earth's octopus but minus the suction cups. Near the ends, the arms 'branch out' into smaller 'fingers'. To hear and speak, I have a diaphragm located on what would be the throat of most Earthly creatures. My eyes are located on short stalks on the top of my head. I breathe through small spiracles located along both sides of my upper body. Eating is accomplished by a mouth located in my single

29

foot, located on the underside of my body; I simply glide over my food and absorb it.

With that out of the way, I should acquaint you with Graak sociology. In his journals, Admiral James has shown some confusion regarding our gender. That is understandable because we have none. The universal translators provided by the Arisians assign masculine pronouns by default and we find it simpler to agree but our language is gender-neutral.

When a Graak finds himself aging, he selects another, usually a friend with suitable genetic traits, and the two exchange 'gene packages'. This is nothing like sexual intercourse and is frequently done openly in public. After the exchange, both parties develop a 'bud' on their bodies which eventually splits away into a new and younger Graak citizen. The original, or 'parent' finds himself rejuvenated. The new or 'child' Graak is capable from the first of independent living but usually stays with the parent for several years, learning the ways of the world. I have budded several times and expect to do so again soon. The good friend and political aide who accompanied me to Earth from Graak was chosen not only for his friendship and political astuteness, he is a good genetic match. It is possible to bud without a gene swap but the young is a genetic copy of the 'parent' and there is no possibility of advancement of the species.

Admiral James was correct about our history. We discovered star flight a very long time ago but did not care to explore far from our home world. We did claim a few planets not far away but failed to mark them clearly. When the Elidorians colonized those same planets, not realizing that we had already claimed them, we attacked. Unable to communicate with the Elidorians, we killed many and captured more. Then we found that we were able to control the Elidorian captives with our minds even though we couldn't communicate. After that, they were in much demand, being large and strong, as well as easy to control. We began raiding their colonies with the express purpose of taking slaves rather than destruction. An attack on their home world was repulsed at great cost to us so we chose not to try that again.

Over the ages, ships from other planets would occasionally visit our world. We were unable to understand their speech so eventually we decided that all outsiders were enemies. We developed a policy of issuing one warning then destroying any ship within our star system.

We modified our starships and even fighter craft to utilize Elidorian pilots with Graak commanders. The Elidorians were capable of faster physical reactions even with Graak brains controlling them. In this way, we developed a type of symbiosis. The Elidorians were not mistreated after capture. Indeed, they seemed happy and content. Our Elidorian, or slave, population flourished.

Then came the advent of the Starship *Enterprise*. That encounter is well and truly told in the book Star Tricks. Needless to say, our

31

planet and culture were nearly destroyed. Fortunately, Captain, now Admiral, James was and is a truly wonderful man. Even after one of our fighters managed to severely wound him, once he had our planet at his mercy, he offered us a way to atone for our past mistakes. He established communications between us and the Elidorians. After that, most of those already on our planet chose to stay as hired employees. They encouraged others to come to work for us. We established trade agreements with Elidoria and those have been a great benefit to both cultures. As a result, both Elidoria and Graak have joined the United Federation of Planets and proudly serve whenever needed.

For myself, I have always loved politics. I served several terms on the Graak World Parliament before choosing adventure with the Space Navy. When my ship, the *Hyperbole*, was damaged in the defense of Earth as related in More Star Tricks, she was repaired at a shipyard near New York City. I was given a tour of the city and fell in love with the city and her people. Not only that, the people seemed to love me. It started as a joke but soon I was a serious candidate for Mayor of New York City. Of course, I was not a resident of New York or even of Earth but the affair set me to thinking. After I returned to Graak, I consulted several of my friends and spoke with many highly placed political figures on Earth. The people of the State of New York wanted me to be their governor. Lawmakers there would push through legislation changing residency requirements and I only needed to immigrate in order to become a legitimate candidate. This required some serious thought but in the end, I resigned my commission in the Graak Space Navy and headed for Earth. In the process, I left my First Officer as Captain of the *Hyperbole*. This was another historic first; he is the first Elidorian to command a Graak ship.

Once on Earth, I set out on a full-blown campaign. The experts told me that my election was all but assured but I didn't want to fail after all this trouble. I'm just not equipped for baby-kissing and many people hesitate to shake my hand but I'm pretty good at speech-making if I do say so myself. I made it a point to know all the political issues that could possibly pertain to the election. I honestly believe that I knew more about the state than the incumbent governor.

Of course, I may have had an unfair advantage. We of Graak do not require sleep. I was able to campaign twenty-four hours out of every day without becoming tired. When no activities were in the offing, I could study. My memory for facts and faces is near-perfect. I can meet a person once in a crowd and then see him next time much later. At that time, I'll remember his name, the names of his wife and children, and the issues that concerned him. This impresses Humans even though it's normal for Graak.

But where does it say that politics must be fair? The same abilities that helped me become governor are the ones that make me a good governor. The people like and trust me and I like the people. There is talk of running me for President of the United States but the Constitution is very difficult to change. As an alternate plan, the World Government has no such residency rules. This will require a lot of thought and study.

The Honorable Vreek,

Governor, State of New York

Planet Earth

NOTE: The next election for World Government will be next year. I'm tempted to hang around Earth just to see what happens.

K. M. J.

CHAPTER III: FREE

This is Freedom Marie James typing. I was born Freedom M. Johnson in Detroit, Michigan to affluent parents along with my identical twin sister, Charlotte.

Daddy was a stockbroker who hit it rich when Scott Montgomery first developed the Monty Car. Daddy somehow guessed right and purchased large blocks of the right stock. He didn't become 'filthy rich' but we lived very well while many others were losing jobs and suffering through the financial readjustments that prevailed for several years.

My mother had delusions of opulence. She wanted to be 'high society' even more than she wanted comfort. Daddy tried hard to keep her happy so he purchased a beautiful house in an upscale neighborhood. He hired a household staff including a handyman-chauffeur, housekeeper, and a series of ladies who were supposed to reign in my sister and myself. None of those ladies lasted long.

In order to maintain our opulent lifestyle, Daddy was forced to work long hours. Mother needed to be a social butterfly, 'lunching' and tennis all day and frequently socializing in the evenings. We girls found that we could easily slip away and make it into a rough section of Detroit where we made friends with a street gang. Mother and Father were mortified and discharged several of our 'keepers' but the next had no better luck. Soon, the gang knew us as 'Free and Easy, the Johnson Twins'.

We were both, however, musically inclined. I took lessons on the piano and ballet while Easy became an accomplished drummer.

By the time we were twelve, we were spending at least three evenings a week 'across the tracks'. Neither of us cared to experiment with drugs but we were both fascinated with sex and beer. This made us extremely popular with the boys. We always had money to buy the beer as long as somebody could go get it. And two identical, willing bodies were always welcome.

Transportation was a problem. Daddy wouldn't let us use any of his Monty Cars even though he owned a small fleet. A taxi would have attracted too much attention in our neighborhood and the walk took a lot of time. We finally reached an accommodation with Daddy's chauffeur, Paul.

Paul, (and that's not his real name) was about thirty at the time and we learned that he was fascinated by our bodies. He caught us experimenting with each other's bodies once and liked what he saw. He said he wouldn't tell if he could see more. After that, we could get him to take us where we wanted if we would give him a show. But over time the show progressed to 'audience participation'. We didn't really mind too much because it proved to us we could handle a grown man and we had unlimited rides. Paul is dead now but we've decided not to drag his name through the mud.

38

When we were just past fourteen, Mother took it into her head to drag us to a debutante ball. It wasn't our 'coming out' party but Mother was determined to outdo everyone else there. She spent a small fortune on dresses, hired the most expensive hairdressers and makeup experts in the state, and insisted that Daddy make everything else perfect. As usual, he said, 'Yes, Dear'.

Daddy's pride and joy was a gasoline-burning stretch limo. Daddy had Paul give it an extra-special cleaning and scour the countryside for enough gasoline for the trip.

"Boss, I got all the gas I could find but the quality isn't good."

"I know it's getting hard to find. Did you try that black market?"

"Yessir. It seems that a bunch of guys are holding drag races using hopped-up gas-burners. There's a big demand for gas lately."

"Did you get enough?"

"It should be enough but we can't afford to waste any."

"Great. How about the route?"

"I scouted it in a Monty Car. The highway from here to there is open but the freeway overpass is barricaded. We'll need to go down the exit, across the freeway, then back up the on ramp."

"Well, with nobody else using the roads, that shouldn't be a problem."

"That's the way I see it."

"All the same, let's leave very early to allow for any problems."

So we left early. The car felt very rough to people accustomed to Monty Cars but there was a feeling of luxury riding in such a large vehicle with the road to ourselves. When we got to the freeway, Paul drove down the ramp and across the southbound lanes. As he crossed the median, the car's engine began to buck and sputter.

"What's wrong, Paul?"

"I don't know, Boss. It acts like it's not getting fuel but there's still plenty showing on the gauge. I better take a look."

So Paul popped the hood and checked the engine. After tinkering a while, he got back behind the wheel.

"Is it fixed?"

"It was a plugged fuel filter. It's a good thing I brought spares."

But just as we started across the northbound lanes, two cars appeared over a rise from our right, bearing down on us at high speed. Paul tried to pull out of the way but the engine died again.

That was the last I remember of it. I was told later that both cars hit us broadside. Mother and Father were killed instantly. Paul was badly injured but lived long enough to call for help on his cell phone. Easy had a terrible head injury and spent the next twenty-four years in a coma. When I finally was aware of my surroundings, I learned that my lower body had been mangled. Both legs had been amputated at mid-thigh and the doctors had been forced to remove my uterus and one of my ovaries.

We had unknowingly driven right in front of a clandestine drag race. Only one of the drag racers survived and he was even more mangled than I. I suppose I could have brought civil action against him but for what purpose? No insurance would cover this and his earning days were over. Fortunately, Daddy had left very good insurance and savings. Along with his stock holdings, I could support Easy and myself for a very long time.

It took much longer than I expected to get out of the hospital. Easy remained for a very long time but they were unable to make any progress with her. I finally hired help and cared for her at home while I attempted to complete my education.

Private duty nurses and home tutors are not inexpensive. At first, I had to lay off the unnecessary household staff then I had to sell the house and move us to a much less expensive address. But no matter what I did, we were bleeding money.

Doing the math, I figured that I could make it through college and Star Fleet Academy and if I could find a suitable nursing home, I could last until I started earning a paycheck. This was all assuming that nothing went wrong.

Yes, adversity forced me to grow up in a hurry. Beer and sex were no longer even on my list of priorities.

Once I managed a high school diploma, I enrolled in a small local college that offered an associate's degree in communications with a minor in computer science. By applying myself assiduously, I graduated with respectable grades. Of course, I didn't take part in the usual college hijinks and my only outside activity was visiting Easy.

While in college, I found living off campus to be more economical than a dorm room. I found a very cheap apartment relatively close to campus but it was in a very rough neighborhood. Of course, I had spent much of my childhood in rough neighborhoods but I didn't know anybody here and now I was in a wheelchair.

Several scary incidents caused me to consider finding a way to defend myself. I contacted several martial arts instructors but all were honest enough to tell me that it would require several years of study before I could possibly become proficient enough to be safe.

In desperation, I decided to buy a gun. I'm a pacifist by nature and the very thought of shooting somebody horrifies me. But the thought of leaving Easy with no family horrifies me more. There was a gun shop along my route to school so one day I stopped in.

Pete Sargent himself was working the counter. I explained my problem and he told me the laws concerning carrying weapons and showed me several small handguns.

"Before you buy anything, you should try it out and see what feels comfortable to you."

He took me to the firing range in the rear of the building and taught me to load a small handgun. He taught me basic safety procedures and how to use the sights.

But the first round I fired went into the ceiling. The second hit the floor. The third hit the right wall. Pete carefully approached me from the rear and retrieved the weapon.

"Maybe you need more instruction."

But no matter how carefully he explained, I couldn't even come close to the target.

"I think with a handgun, you'd be more of a danger to yourself than your enemies."

I had to agree.

"Let's try a rifle."

He handed me a rifle that looked familiar from TV.

43

"This is a Colt AR-15. It's the civilian version of the military M-16 and will do all the same things except fire on fully automatic mode."

He showed me the safety and how to use the sights. After reviewing safety precautions, he had me try to fire it.

I lined up the sights, took a deep breath, and squeezed the trigger.

There was a sharp 'crack' and a hole appeared in the target exactly where I had been aiming.

"Try another one."

I went through an entire magazine and every round went right where I wanted.

"I think we've found the weapon for you."

"But this is pretty hard to conceal and it will attract a lot of attention lying in my lap."

"I have an idea about that. If you'll keep practicing with this, I'll work on something. Give me a week."

So every day for a week, I stopped by the shop and fired a couple boxes of ammunition. After a while, I found that I didn't even need to use the sights; I just seemed to hit the target by instinct.

Early the next week when I stopped by, Pete had a different wheelchair for me.

"What's this?"

"This was in a pawnshop down the street. I picked it up cheap and made some modifications. Let me help you change chairs."

The new chair was even more comfortable than my old one but the arms seemed bigger and bulkier than usual.

"Let's take it back to the firing range. I want to show you something."

Pressing a hidden release on the right armrest caused it to come free. Another button caused the entire arm to break free of the chair. When I snapped the armrest to what had been the front of the chair arm, the entire thing became a strange-looking but very functional rifle. When I fitted it to my shoulder, it felt a lot like my familiar AR-15.

"The other chair arm holds spare magazines."

"So this is a concealed AR-15?"

"Well, I cheated a little. There's an extra click on the safety and it'll fire a three-round burst. It's usually a waste of ammo but it can be handy if you need to get somebody's attention."

"Is this legal to carry?"

"Of course not. But you probably wouldn't have managed a concealed weapon permit anyway and this is far better for you than a pistol."

"It's a better wheelchair too. My old one was about worn out."

"All part of the service, Ma'am."

The custom rifle wasn't cheap but Pete tossed in the wheelchair free. He also allowed me to use his firing range free of charge and gave me a big discount on practice ammunition.

My friends at school admired my new chair. Of course, I didn't tell anybody about its extra features, only that it was a present from a friend.

One late evening a few months later, I was returning from visiting Easy. I didn't own a Monty Car then and relied on public transportation so I had to wheel myself about three blocks home.

As I passed the entrance to an alley near Pete's gun shop, a man stepped out and grabbed my wheelchair from behind. Before I could react, I was in the alley and surrounded by men I didn't recognize. They were at that dangerous stage of drunkenness where they still had a fair amount of physical coordination but very little common sense. They had decided they wanted a woman and I happened along at precisely the wrong time. I believe the wheelchair was an added 'turnon' to them.

They were between me and the exit to the alley so I broke away and headed deeper into the alley. After about one hundred feet, I found that I had guessed wrong. The alley was

46

a dead end and the crazy drunks had me cornered.

Apparently they knew I couldn't get away because they weren't even hurrying. They were chugging beer, high-fiving each other and wandering in my direction.

I didn't want to hurt anybody but I didn't want to let myself be hurt either. I quickly assembled my rifle and let them see what I had in my hands.

It appeared that they weren't impressed. They continued to advance on me and I feared I would be forced to kill the lot of them.

Then I had an inspiration. I switched the rifle's safety to the third position and pulled the trigger. The rifle fired three fast rounds into the air mimicking the machine guns you often hear on TV.

This was precisely the attention grabber I needed. The drunks suddenly decided that their interests were somewhere else. In only a matter of seconds, I could stow my rifle and continue my interrupted journey home.

That was about the only significant event of my college years. Other than that, I went to class, studied, and visited Easy. I had focused on a career with Star Fleet and I would let nothing interfere. The adventure and very good pay with benefits sounded great to me.

The media had been running ads for some time wanting specialists in many different categories. The famous Scott Montgomery was building a starship and would need a crew. After that, more ships were planned so he was founding a training school for officers. Star Fleet Academy required a minimum of a bachelor of arts in specific fields. The first class would be short but after that, the entire course was expected to be two years. Pay and benefits for a Star Fleet officer were far more than I could ever expect to make on Earth. I estimated that I would be making enough to support Easy while exploring the galaxy.

I was accepted by Star Fleet Academy despite my physical limitations. Apparently my preparation and qualifications offset my handicap. Since I was applying to be a Communications Officer, mobility on the job would not be a major factor.

Classes at Star Fleet Academy did, however, require me to move around quickly and I finally found myself forced to purchase a used battery powered wheelchair. Since I was living on campus just outside Iowa City, Iowa, I was relatively safe but I missed my 'concealed weapon'.

The first accelerated course at Star Fleet Academy was originally scheduled to last one year but shortly after classes began, it was announced that the ship we were training to 'crew' was ahead of schedule so more unnecessary subjects were being dropped from the curriculum and we would be graduating in

48

six months. After our class, the course would be two years. However, the next two classes wound up being accelerated also as ships were being completed faster than crews. Mr. Montgomery, whom I now know very well as my brother-in-law, Scotty, is an extremely intelligent man but sometimes his patience is not the best.

So our class had a full crew ready when the *Enterprise* passed her test flights. I had scored the highest in the communications field so I was given the coveted position of Red Watch Communications Officer. Learning of my disability and need to use a powered wheelchair, Mr. Montgomery had the Communications seat rigged to be easily removed and replaced in order to make room for my chair.

My quarters needed no modification. I had learned to get by in a world adapted for people with legs. The ability to reduce the gravity in the bathroom was a luxury I had never even imagined. Showers were a pleasure instead of a trial. I merely needed to keep enough gravity so that the water found the drain.

When I met the captain of the ship, I nearly fell out of my chair. I suppose not all women would think so but I considered the man to be absolutely gorgeous. He was white, (And don't give me that stuff about black women not being attracted to white men) about six feet tall, around one hundred seventy pounds with balding dark brown hair and the prettiest blue eyes I ever saw.

I honestly hadn't touched a man since before the accident that took my legs at the age of fourteen. At first, I hurt too much then I just didn't want to be bothered. Meeting Captain Kirk James stirred feelings I thought were gone forever. I tried not to let him know how I felt; it just doesn't do to be 'needy'.

Captain James was a fine leader of people too. He very rarely raised his voice but had a way of making everyone want to do as he wanted. It just seemed as if what he said was the perfect thing to do. I never saw or heard anyone resist or refuse one of his orders. You always felt that you were working WITH him, not FOR him.

I'm not going to describe our adventures those first few months; Kirk did an excellent job in his journals published as Star Tricks, More Star Tricks, etc. About all I have to add is my part when Kirk was wounded in our 'contact difficulties' with the Graak. As he was lying on the control room floor bleeding, I was overcome with a rage I had never felt before. Then I realized that I had a duty to Kirk and the ship. I was the highest ranking officer present so that left me in charge.

"Screwloose, get that fighter."

I rushed to Kirk's side and applied a tourniquet to the bleeding stump of his right wrist.

"Wrongway, call Spock, Damage control, and an emergency medical team to the bridge."

When Spock arrived, he could see that I was barely holding myself together so he called his Gold Watch Communications Officer to relieve me. Once he arrived, I broke down in tears and the medical officer had another patient.

But when I reported for my next watch, things were subtly different. Everyone treated me differently. What would previously have elicited an 'Okay, Free' now got me a 'Yes, Ma'am'. No amount of begging would change things back. Even Spock started treating me like a serious officer. He had always been rather polite and formal but now he was even more respectful. Later, when Kirk promoted me, all I heard was applause and approval. I guess some of Kirk is rubbing off on me and it's possible to be an effective leader without being a 'military clown'.

Let me tell you about Scotty. He was an enigma to me for a long time. Scotty is a good-looking man but he's always rumpled and rarely cares how he looks. When I first came aboard the *Enterprise,* I would catch occasional glimpses of him and had trouble reconciling the actuality with the legend.

One day, he flagged me down as I left the bridge after a watch.

"Do you have any plans this evening?"

"Only dinner." I thought he was 'coming on' to me. I wasn't really interested in romance, having promised myself to make Kirk the first man in my new life.

"I had an inspiration for a new type of prosthetic leg. I believe that you would be the perfect person to try them out if you're willing to help me."

"I won't break my neck with this, will I?"

"They have safety fields to protect you."

"Let's give 'em a try."

So I started spending most of my evenings in Scotty's lab. The new legs looked a lot like a panty girdle with small electronic packages in several spots. But when activated, I could walk for the first time in twenty-four years! It took practice but I had been walking on my stumps around my apartment for a long time and my balance was good. Scotty had included a balancing field so it was nearly impossible to fall, too. Altogether, it only took about a month of practice and fine-tuning before we both agreed I was ready. Kirk tells that story in Star Tricks too.

I now have several sets of 'legs'. They're easily cleaned in a Montgomery washer and at the first sign of electronic difficulties, I take them in for a checkup.

So I chose the correct career and if I had delayed long enough to get another ship, things would have been very different. Even Easy's 'rescue' wouldn't have happened if I hadn't been on the same ship as Spock. In all, I owe my wonderful life to my darling husband, Kirk M. James.

NOTE: I really didn't ask people to say nice things about me. And I didn't edit these autobiographies. If somebody says something rotten about me, I'll let you see that, too.

Kirk M. James

CHAPTER IV: Spock

I am S'ponkavonvetchakinaian. Those of you who have been reading the journals written by Admiral James will know me as Spock. My formal name is a recitation of the names of my ancestors for six generations and listing their important accomplishments. To speak that name requires nearly a full day and would need many printed pages. When I began associating with Humans, they found even my common name difficult so they began calling me Spock after a popular television character.

Admiral James has asked me to write about my early life. This may be difficult as my people are much longer-lived than Humans and there were many events that shaped the person who now writes this missive.

As I am writing this essentially for Human edification, I should tell you about my people. We are born with vestigial organs for both sexes but neither gender is functional. We remain in this state until we choose to mate, based on friendship and intellectual admiration. Once two persons choose to mate, they decide which gender role each will take and their bodies change to suit that role. This is not accomplished quickly or easily and in most cases a person will remain the same gender for life.

While we have no formal institution of marriage, pair-bonding is usually for life. Even after the children are grown and the parents are past child-bearing age, they are so accustomed to each other and their gender roles that they remain together for life.

In my case, I mated very early; I bonded at an age that would correspond to about thirty years of age in a Human and chose the female role. My male partner was an explorer and was gone exploring the galaxy in a spaceship much more than he was home. Perhaps that is the reason I never bore children. One day, his ship returned without him. After a time, my body reverted to its genderless state or 'nominal male'.

But my mate's stories of the galaxy had intrigued me. I enrolled in the Academy of Science and began studying subjects that would qualify me to go with the exploring ships.

To describe the Academy of Science, there is nothing like it on Earth. It is rather like a university but many degrees of magnitude larger than any on Earth. Our Academy is larger than New York City and although its population constantly changes, it houses several million students.

On my home world, we have very little mechanical transportation. We certainly have the technology to build it but prefer to walk most of the time. Therefore, it is common practice to find temporary lodgings near a student's classes.

56

Classes are scheduled in blocks near together so students are easily able to attend without hurrying.

One of my favorite subjects was alien languages. Long ago, the ships had discovered a planet that the inhabitants called Earth in the primary language. That primary language was called English and I seemed to have an affinity for it. Exploring ships had brought back many recordings in English and I became very proficient in translating them. Others who understood English said my accent was perfect.

Another required subject was emergency medicine. This was a long course and I chose to take a temporary residence near the class building. I managed to find accommodations with another student who was to become a lifelong friend.

Technopraunicnorianiachoignialian was studying medicine, not to become a physician but simply because it interested him. He was already employed as a computer programmer but was taking a sabbatical for study and relaxation.

During my extended stay with him, we became very good friends. We often sat up late at night discussing current events, history, and many other subjects.

After completing my studies, I was offered a position on a ship that was to visit Earth. My knowledge of the English language

57

would be valuable and the United States was of particular interest on this voyage.

When we arrived on Earth, the conflict known as World War One was in progress. As mentioned, we mostly visited the United States but did look in on activities in Europe. The violence shocked and horrified me. How can otherwise intelligent people do such things?

This was the first of my many visits to Earth. I became fascinated with the planet and its people. I would have been happy to make contact but many of my people feared Humans and refused to make the attempt. Later, only the inability to locate a suitable new planet for our population forced my people to agree. That story is told in Star Tricks.

On our visits to Earth, we did our best to remain inconspicuous but as Earth sciences improved, our ships began to attract attention. Tales of 'flying saucers' often resulted from our visits although we never did any of the things reported; we never kidnapped anyone or created 'crop circles' and it is not our ship, if any, housed in Area fifty-one.

When I returned to my home planet, I once again contacted my friend Technopraunicnorianiachoignialian. He was now employed as a programmer for medical computer systems. Because I expected to be leaving frequently on exploration voyages, we decided to share lodgings. During the times I was at home, our friendship grew and somehow, it also grew while I was away.

As this was happening, astrophysicists were becoming increasingly alarmed about the condition of our world's star. We had known for many generations that the star was nearing nova stage but recently it had shown signs of rapid deterioration. Scientists now said the end was very near. The political leaders made an unusually hasty decision and dispatched a ship to Earth with instructions to request assistance. I was chosen to go on this voyage because of my mastery of the English language. The full story of this planetary rescue is told in the book Star Tricks.

But the rapidity of this decision caused considerable confusion in my personal life. For a long time, Technopraunicnorianiachoignialian and I had been discussing becoming mates. He had always imagined himself as a female while I had experience as a female. We had not decided which of us was to be the male partner when I found that I must leave abruptly. When I returned much ahead of schedule aboard the *Enterprise*, Technopraunicnorianiachoignialian was away visiting family members so we were unable to continue the discussion.

The next time I heard from Technopraunicnorianiachoignialian, he had become female and changed his name to the Human-use name, T'prau. He, or now she, had acted on the assumption that I would become the male partner.

I care enough for T'prau that I continued with a Human-style wedding.

Details can be found in Star Tricks.

My life continued happily from that point. I was pleased and surprised when Admiral James asked me to be captain of the *Enterprise*. Not only had I never considered myself a powerful leader, no non-Human had ever commanded an Earth starship before. However, the crew and the remainder of Star Fleet accepted me and I found myself comfortable in the position. T'prau shows great pride in my accomplishments and I find myself quite content in the position.

Despite his misgivings, Admiral James has proven himself to be the outstanding leader the Galactic Fleet needs. His instinctive leadership by example and simple good sense make him the person to whom all instinctively look for answers. When I find myself facing a difficult decision, I base my answer on what I believe Admiral James would do.

NOTE: What is this, the Kirk James Admiration Society? I was counting on Spock to say something rotten about me. Well, there are several people to go, stay tuned.

Kirk James

CHAPTER V: SCOTTY

Kirk asked me to write about myself. I hate talking about myself and I rarely write anything but here goes.

I'm Scott Raymond Montgomery. Don't blame me for that; nobody asked my opinion at the time and by the time I was even aware of the name, it was already officially recorded. In later years, when Star Trek made the name Montgomery Scott a household word, I took a lot of 'ribbing', especially since my best friend was named Kirk James. I just developed a Scottish accent to go with the name. This no doubt sounded especially odd coming from the only black kid in the entire county.

Kirk and I have been friends as long as either of us can remember. Our parents were friends before we were born and we were raised as almost-brothers from the very first. I can't remember a significant event in my life that didn't involve Kirk and usually his parents.

My parents were originally from Chicago. They fell in love and I was the result. This turned out to be a problem; in those days, mixed-race marriages just weren't accepted and Dad couldn't bear to walk away from Mom as was common practice in those days when a white boy got a black girl pregnant. Neither family would accept the marriage and the two found themselves shunned everywhere they went. Dad was even unable to find suitable work.

Then Dad heard that work and acceptance could be found in California. All he had was an old jalopy of a car and a few dollars but he and Mom decided to try. Finding a friendly minister to make their marriage legal, they loaded up and headed west.

They were barely across the Mississippi River when the car began showing signs of serious trouble. Dad managed to coax it along for quite a few miles but knew it would not reach California without major repairs. He picked a small town at random and stopped, hoping to earn some money.

There, he had the first stroke of really good luck he'd had in many years. He met Patrick James. Patrick was an electrical engineer for a local agricultural equipment manufacturing company and he needed some work done on his house. Patrick hired Dad for the job and was very pleased with the work. He recommended Dad to everyone he knew and soon Dad had more work than he could do. This turned into such a business that Dad opened a full-time shop and settled down in that small Iowa town. Even after his death, the business still prospers as 'Let George Do It' and handles all kinds of handyman jobs.

As for Dad and Patrick, of course they became great friends and raised their sons, Kirk

64

and I, together. After my parents were killed in an automobile accident when I was twelve, Kirk's parents became my foster parents and continued taking care of me until I graduated college.

During our formative years, Kirk and I were the terror of our little town. We never did anything criminally wrong but most 'orneriness' involved us. Kirk tells a lot of it very well in Star Tricks.

Earlier, I mentioned Star Trek. I've always been a 'nut' about technology in general and loved reading and watching science fiction. When Star Trek came on TV, you couldn't pry me away. Even the 'ribbing' I got about the name coincidence failed to dampen my enthusiasm.

One thing about sci-fi that always fascinated me was the 'force fields' that most of the shows seemed to take for granted. How did they work? How were they generated? I made it my personal mission to find out. All during my studies in electronic engineering, I watched for applications that might be useful but with little success. After I was employed as an electronic engineer, I spent a lot of my spare time experimenting with the concept.

Then one night I had a dream. In the dream an odd circuit diagram impressed itself on my mind. When I woke, I carefully drew the circuit on a piece of paper so I wouldn't forget it. Putting the paper away, I went to work.

Of course, I had a hectic day at work then plans that evening. One thing led to another and that scrap of paper didn't come to my attention again for several months.

Then one evening I had nothing particular to do. Kirk was coming over to use my computer and I wanted to tinker around in my garage lab while he did it. As I was changing out of my work clothes, I came across that scrap of paper and decided to try that circuit. I had all necessary components on hand so I got right to work. That's another story Kirk tells in Star Tricks but it was the beginning of my success. That force field turned into a star drive and many other applications. It became a cure for cancer and most other diseases. It became many other medical miracles. The list of things that can be done with variations on that circuit would fill books. And I managed to patent and license most of them. I do, however, refuse to make a profit on medical applications; I don't need the money and the patients need the applications.

I really didn't set out to become nearly as wealthy as things turned out. Of course, I wanted to be rich but I just wanted to be middlin' rich. I learned the hard way that extreme wealth involves extreme responsibility.

Once my 'Monty Cars' replaced gasoline powered vehicles, many people found themselves jobless. I held myself responsible for this so I decided to do something about it. I used a lot of my money opening new businesses with the specific intent of putting people to work. I encouraged old-fashioned craftsmanship over automation. Some of my business managers objected, quoting efficiency statistics but I countered by suggesting that they could become statistics themselves.

Of course, one project that was near and dear to my heart was the construction of a starship. I hired many futuristic-thinking designers and engineers and then refurbished a couple defunct automobile manufacturing facilities. I hired a lot of people and it took years but finally the *Enterprise* was ready.

Since I had all the facilities in place, I had them start on more ships. Many people had shown an interest in space and Star Fleet Academy had many more applicants than the *Enterprise* could possibly use so more ships seemed a logical answer. I was still raking in money in embarrassingly large chunks and this seemed a good way to use it. It's against my basic nature to waste money but I don't mind spending it for what I consider to be a good cause.

Kirk has already told of our adventures in Star Tricks so I won't go into that.

You may note that I mention Kirk a lot. Even though I developed the field that powers the ship and is the basis for most of the advanced technology we use, I couldn't possibly have done it without Kirk. His leadership and level headed control of every situation have proven to be exactly what the entire galaxy needs. I'm very happy to be associated with such a man.

NOTE: *Et Tu,* Scotty? I was hoping for at least one bad rap from you.

Kirk James

CHAPTER VI: M'bing

Hello, my name is M'Bing and I am originally from the planet Ecostria. I suppose I should begin by telling you about the people of my planet and how we look since many of you may not have seen any of us.

Since immigrating to Earth, I have had occasion to read a lot of your literature and I was impressed by some of your classic fiction. In some of the tales, there are descriptions of creatures called centaurs. In Greek mythology, the centaur was a creature composed of a Human torso joined to a horse's withers. As an Ecostrian, I am shaped very much like that but while my upper body is shaped generally like a Human's, I would not be confused with a Human if I were photographed from the chest up. I possess essentially the same features but I do not resemble a Human in facial configuration. My lower body is slightly larger than an Earthly pony but smaller than a horse. All higher forms of life on my home world possess six limbs but in most, all six are used for locomotion.

To further describe Ecostria, the planet itself was long ago nearly split in half by an asteroid collision. By some miracle, the two halves remained in contact but with a huge rift splitting the planet at roughly the equator. For all of our recorded history, we have been unable to reach the southern half of the planet and even

71

now, with modern transportation, we have found the southern half of our world to be uninhabitable.

The northern half is moderately populated with many cities of varying sizes. We have what we considered advanced technology but did not discover energy-gathering fields on our own. That was forced on us and I'll explain that in a moment.

On our world, there are no flying creatures. Not even flying insects. Plants exchange genetic information using crawling insects or by spreading pollen on the air. Perhaps because of this or for some other reason, we never developed the fascination with the sky that many others did. While we have had efficient ground transportation for a very long time, it never occurred to us to fly. Likewise, astronomy was never an interest to us; the stars were simply pretty lights in the night sky. We were never simple people; our interests just lay in other directions.

Our industry developed very early due to a mineral that was and still is plentiful on our world. This mineral burns easily and very cleanly, providing originally steam power then generating electricity after its discovery. Combustion of this mineral produces only carbon dioxide and water with no pollution so we were spared the ecological nightmares Earth faced by using hydrocarbons.

72

My father and his father before him were in the business of installing and repairing electrical generators that were powered by this mineral. Naturally, I went into the business and was prospering in it well into my middle years until one day we were 'visited' by beings from outer space.

As I mentioned, we had never even thought of the stars as habitats for other beings. When spaceships landed, it was what your people call 'culture shock'. The 'visitors' were of two varieties: large, two-legged beings called Feraldi and smaller two-legged beings called Picaldu. Both varieties were determined to take our natural resources and didn't even wish to do the work of collecting them. They set about forcing our people to work, enslaving us by threat and violence. Any resistance was met with death and destruction.

We have never been a warlike people. Armed conflict just wasn't known on our world and hunting wasn't a popular sport so very few weapons were available and few of us had a clue about fighting.

Nevertheless, we decided to resist these invaders as well as we may. Resistance organizations were formed but we had no idea how to do such things. Individual invaders sometimes 'disappeared' but such incidents frequently aroused the wrath of the invaders.

I was leading a local resistance group in my home city. One day, a police officer

73

contacted me, telling me that some visitors were present but did not seem to be of the sort we were fighting. Since I had some experience with the Feraldi and Picaldu, could I speak with them?

When I arrived, it was apparent that these were another type of people entirely. Upon speaking with them, I learned that these visitors were from the United Federation of Planets and led by Captain Kirk James. These people were here to help us.

And help they did. Captain (now Admiral) James was and is the finest leader and the best friend I have ever known. He and his people not only defended us, they showed us how to defend ourselves. By the time our world was free of unwanted guests, we were well able to protect ourselves and we now possessed the technology the invaders had left behind. Federation technical advisors remained on our planet to teach us the use of our new-found technology.

My electrical generating business was now obsolete, a victim of the new energy-gathering fields. Having nothing better to do, I volunteered for the newly-formed space navy and found myself the captain of a former Feraldi starship.

Later, when Earth was attacked by misguided forces from the Andromeda galaxy, our ships joined with the remainder of the Federation fleet in Earth's defense. My ship was damaged in the abortive battle and needed repairs on Earth. During those repairs I met Daisy.

Daisy is the most wonderful creature on any planet in any galaxy. She's a pony but not just any pony. She's beautiful, smart, and witty.

I had gone to a local horse and pony ranch near the Star Fleet repair facility for some exercise and was running in the field when I found myself running next to Daisy. Once we started talking, I knew we had to find a way to be together forever.

I went over to the rancher to see what could be done and was surprised to learn that he had never heard Daisy speak before. It seemed that Humans and equestrians had never been able to communicate until my presence made it possible. With me nearby and the translator supplied by the Arisians, he could talk with any of the ponies or horses.

The rancher wanted me to remain in his employ but my ship needed me for at least the trip home. After some bargaining, one of my crew agreed to remain on Earth at an extremely high salary and exchange for Daisy. In the end, all parties felt they had received good value.

Captain James, on learning of this, introduced me to his brother, Dick, who owns and operates a horse and pony ranch in Wyoming. Upon hearing what I could do, Dick offered me full-time employment on his ranch, merely to facilitate communication with his animals. This, of course would start after I returned my ship to Ecostria and Daisy and I were married there. Daisy and I discussed it and decided this sounded like the best future we could plan.

The Bar-Be-Cute is the most beautiful place I have ever seen. The scenery is spectacular and Dick, along with his lovely wife Rita, operate the ranch wonderfully. Daisy tells me that the winters are more severe than those she was accustomed to in Iowa but the ranch has Montgomery fields that shield the pastures and buildings from most of the worst of it. Some cold and snow are allowed in for ecological reasons.

The ranch hands are a jovial bunch and were extremely happy when I joined the group. My presence made it possible for them to actually communicate with the ponies and horses in their care and that made their job much easier. Now, instead of forcing an animal to do as they wished, they merely needed to ask. And if the animal has a problem, he or she can voice it through me. Dick was so impressed that he had me send word to Ecostria and he hired two handicapped Ecostrians who were unable to find meaningful employment at home but were perfectly suited for the job here. Other local ranchers followed suit and now there are several Ecostrians nearby.

As for me, I love my job, I love this ranch, I love Earth, and I love Daisy. What else could I want? I owe this all to Admiral Kirk James. I've been reading his exploits and it appears that his career as Fleet Admiral is going well also. The man deserves any accolade or award that anyone cares to bestow upon him. I wish him the very best.

NOTE: I hope nobody proposes me for sainthood; I think I need to be dead first.

Kirk James

CHAPTER VII: Colena

Hello, Kirk asked me to write about myself and I reluctantly agreed.

My name is Colena and I'm originally from the planet Meena in what is now the Enterprisian Star Cluster. When I was born, the Star Cluster was an Empire ruled by an Emperor called Nurga. At that time, the Empire was known as Roatta but when I was in my teens, a new Emperor took the throne.

This new Emperor's name was Klug and he renamed the Empire after himself.

Life under Nurga was oppressive but it was even worse under Klug.

My planet, Meena, was ruled locally by a viceroy appointed by the Emperor and this viceroy ruled with an iron hand. The one appointed by Nurga had restricted education and exercised control over most areas of private life but Klug's viceroy took these matters to a new extreme.

Nearly always when there is an unpopular and oppressive government, you will find an underground resistance movement. Meena was no exception. My entire family was heavily involved with the local chapter of the resistance.

79

Not long after Klug's viceroy took power, my parents and brother were arrested by the secret police during a raid of a resistance meeting. I would have been caught also but I had been delayed in attending. My father and brother were sent to a labor camp where I later learned that they perished building the viceroy's new home. My mother was enslaved in the home of a friend of the viceroy.

So I was left to fend for myself at the age of sixteen. There were no social programs in place to assist me but many others were aware of my situation and helped with food, clothing, and shelter. Since the secret police frequently checked on household populations, I could not stay permanently with any particular family but I could be a frequent 'visitor'.

One day, after being flushed from one home by a 'census taker', I was on my way to another family when I came upon a man being accosted by two policemen. As far as I could see, the man had done nothing wrong; the policemen just didn't like the way he looked.

The man being accosted was about average size but stood with a bent posture and appeared frail in his long grey hooded robe. He leaned heavily on a heavy staff longer than he was tall as the policemen berated him for his appearance and anything else they could think of.

Local police were recruited from the largest and crudest men the viceroy could find.

Intelligence was definitely not a prerequisite. Their job was to strut around in their flashy uniforms and 'keep the people in line' with little regard to actual laws. They were armed with a deadly sidearm and a force blade each. The sidearm could fire a beam capable of burning a hole through a person or most objects. The force blade was a handle long enough to be held in two hands. When activated, it projected a beam about two meters long and about one molecule thick. This 'blade' was extremely rigid and sharp and could slice nearly any material effortlessly.

I made up my mind to help the old man if I possibly could. I edged closer, waiting for an opportunity.

Then one of the policemen made a serious mistake. He tried to shove the old man. The old man barely moved but the policeman sailed over the old man's head and landed heavily on his back. After a shocked moment, the other policeman drew his force blade and activated it. The old man picked up his fallen staff and with a few lightning-fast moves, knocked the force blade from the policeman's hand.

Dropping his staff again, the old man advanced on the policeman. In a blur of motion, his hands and feet seemed to hit the policeman everywhere at once. In less time than it takes to tell it, the policeman was unconscious.

81

"Sir, do you need help?" I really did want to help him.

"Yes, Girl. Get the other cop's weapons and we'll get out of here before they wake up."

I did exactly as I was told. This was not a man to disobey.

"Sir, where are we going?" We were now quite some distance from the fallen police officers.

"We are going to my school. I am a teacher of dance. Be certain to keep those weapons hidden; the police kill civilians with any kind of weapon."

I clutched more tightly at my roll of clothing with the weapons hidden inside.

As we walked he asked how I came to be out on my own and I told him my story.

"Perhaps you can help me. The young lady who was working for me recently got married and moved away. I need someone to clean my dance studio. The job doesn't pay much but it includes food and a place to live. Are you interested?"

So I went to work cleaning the dance studio. It wasn't long before I learned that dancing was only a small part of what Yunga taught. At odd hours, he taught members of the resistance movement how to fight, both unarmed and with ancient weapons that didn't look like weapons.

Yunga proved to be a master of Chinga-Con, an ancient martial art that few people knew anything about but with proper training, a person could become an incredible fighter. Since becoming exposed to some of Earth's martial arts, I've noticed many similarities to the Chinese styles.

Soon, I was receiving lessons as part of my pay. By applying my work as training, I managed to strengthen my muscles even more quickly than I expected. Yunga prepared the food himself and while his choices seemed strange, they were exactly what I needed to develop my body properly.

Within four years, Yunga had me teaching classes. He told me that I was approaching the point of being a master of the style. He said he had never taught a better pupil. Of course, I had done nothing in all that time but clean, study, and train.

Chinga-Con is an ancient art that utilizes weapons such as swords. Of course, the viceroy forbade the possession of swords but Yunga had several he only brought out for training purposes. He taught me the forbidden techniques and after long practice he told me I seemed to be a natural at the art. Together, we modified sword techniques to the use of captured force blades.

Meanwhile, the revolution was intensifying all over the Star Cluster. One day Yunga asked to speak with me.

"Grand daughter, General Multa has asked me to come to his training base on an unnamed planet. There, he is training an army to fight the Emperor's forces. But I am too old for such traveling and I prefer to remain here. I answered that I would send my most trusted and competent senior student in my place. That student, My Dear, is you. Will you do this for me?"

"But Grandfather, as you said, you need help here. Who will clean the dance studio and help teach the students?"

"Famala can clean and Jamal will help teach. This revolution is important and we all must do our part in any way we can."

"But Famala is nearly as old as you and Jamal is blind."

"I have spoken with both and they feel it is their duty to the greater good of all to allow you to assist the revolution."

"Then I will do as you ask. Tell the General that I will come."

"I am very proud of you, Colena. You have worked and studied very hard and I believe that you are as least as good at Chinga-Con as I

84

ever was. Train the General's troops well; they are the hope of the entire Star Cluster."

That was the last time I saw Yunga. On the day the revolution succeeded, he suffered a heart attack and passed away. Jamal continued to operate the martial arts school but now without the disguise of dance. Despite his blindness, he is still legendary as a teacher.

When I arrived on the unnamed training planet, I was issued uniforms as a member of the Revolutionary Army. I was surprised to learn that I was suddenly a high-ranking sergeant. I would be in charge of teaching unarmed combat and my supervisor would be a young Lieutenant named Kawa.

There was no time to teach the recruits all the techniques of Chinga-Con so I condensed the course into basic hand-to-hand fighting. I believe that the people I trained were better able to defend themselves if they must fight unarmed and the general seemed satisfied with my curriculum.

Off-duty, Lieutenant Kawa and I became VERY close friends. In all these years, I had never had time for any kind of romance or even a serious flirtation so I learned a lot from him. I wasn't in love but it was a strong case of 'like'.

General Multa, being a very smart commander, didn't have all of his troops on a single planet. When his headquarters world was

85

attacked, the Empire missed our training planet. The Revolutionary Army lost many seasoned troops and a lot of hardware but we had three classes of new troops in various stages of training.

Shortly after this, General Multa decided to strike a blow in return. He sent for Lieutenant Kawa and me.

"I know that the two of you are supposed to be training new recruits but I need experts to rescue a couple of very important people. I just learned of the location of our true queen and queen mother. I would like you, Kawa, to lead an elite squad in an assault on the residence where they are being held. Colena, I would like you to lead the squad that will escort the queen and her mother to safety. While you are doing this, the remainder of our fleet will be engaging the Imperial fleet a long distance from the planet where the queen is being held. I will provide you with detailed plans of the residence and allow you to work out the details. Will you do it?"

Of course we did it. And it was the beginning of the Enterprisian Hostage Rescue Unit. Lieutenant (now General) Kawa had found his true calling. After the revolution, Queen Colata formed the Enterprisian Marine Corps and the Hostage Rescue Unit had an esteemed place there.

A much more complete telling of the story of the revolution can be found in many

86

history books or in Admiral James's book Star Tricks.

More recently, Queen Colata passed away giving birth to Admiral James's son, whom she named James. As her son, James, is the hereditary king of the Enterprisian Star Cluster. Of course, he is far too young to effectively rule so Colata's Consort, Marana, is holding the throne as Stewardess until James reaches the age of majority at seventeen. I was granted the extreme honor of becoming his bodyguard and governess. I take this duty very seriously and love the little boy as if he is my own son. As he becomes older, I intend to teach him Chinga-Con, both in order to defend himself if necessary and for the self discipline it will help him learn.

Kirk, Admiral James, visits when he can but his duties to the entire galaxy are manifold. I don't think there is a woman or near-woman in the entire galaxy who wouldn't throw herself at his feet; myself included. But the man seems oblivious to his charms. Perhaps that's part of his charm. I only wish more men were like him.

NOTE: Come on, isn't there at least one person out there who hates me? Maybe if Marvin were still alive.......

Kirk James

CHAPTER VIII: Easy

Hello, I'm Charlotte Christine Montgomery but my maiden name was Johnson. Freedom James and I are identical twin sisters and I managed to read her earlier entry so I'll try to omit a lot of the details you already read. This will no doubt cause my submission to be fairly short but I promised Kirk so here goes:

Growing up fairly wealthy in Detroit is not a terrible life but we came to strongly dislike it. I suppose we would have hated any life that involved our social-climbing mother. She was never satisfied with what she had and always strove to appear richer and more refined than she actually was. Poor Daddy was driven to distraction attempting to keep her happy. We didn't actually hate Mother; we were more embarrassed for her than anything else. I suppose our rebellion was more our way of protesting than anything else.

Of course, at the time, we saw our rebellion as 'growing up', no matter how childish it truly was. It truly is amazing that neither of us became seriously injured, diseased, or in trouble with the law.

Our juvenile hedonistic lifestyle was fun, however, and at that age, fun is the name of the game. Mother had no real idea what we were doing and Daddy was too busy trying to support

Mother's social fantasies. The various nannies and governesses were all too easily outwitted and thus eliminated from the game. The only adult who really understood us was 'Paul' and he was his own kind of problem.

As I mentioned, Paul had no illusions about us.

Free and I had learned at a very early age that playing with each other's body was more pleasurable than playing with our own.

Not long after we had managed to slip away to meet a group of boys in a rough section of town, we were trying to decide how to do it again without the long walk. The fantasizing about the sexual games with the boys progressed to playing together. Paul happened to look in and caught us.

We begged Paul not to tell our parents, fearing punishment. He told us he wouldn't tell if we would continue what we were doing and allow him to watch. We countered with an offer to allow him to watch if he would drive us on occasional 'excursions' into town.

This set a pattern that continued for quite some time. However, after a while, Paul began touching us and the touching escalated into much more serious contact. Even though we were very young, we enjoyed the contact and never even thought of complaining to anyone.

90

Paul wasn't doing anything we weren't doing with the boys downtown and we were actually flattered.

From my present adult viewpoint, Paul was certainly a child molester and should have been reported to the authorities but he has been dead for many years and a promise is a promise. He no doubt has a surviving family so Free and I have chosen not to reveal his true name to avoid embarrassing them.

After the accident, my memory is very fragmented. I was not totally unaware of my surroundings but I believe that I 'faded in and out' for a very long time. I was unable to control even my eyes so it was only occasionally that they happened to be directed properly to see what I wished. My mind was the only thing under my control so I spent a lot of time withdrawn, largely ignoring the outside world while I dreamed or spun fantasies.

I would, however, emerge from my 'shell' when Free visited. Her presence was always worth my attention, even when my body was painful from the therapy administered to prevent muscle atrophy.

When Free tearfully told me she was going away on the *USS Enterprise*, I wanted to kiss her. I couldn't expect my condition to ever improve and she needed to have a life of her own, not tied to mine.

After that, I withdrew for a long time. I knew Free would be back some day but until then, I had little to interest me.

Then one day I was re-replaying a scene from the past, embellishing as much as my imagination would allow when Free's voice penetrated. Was she really here or was this a new fantasy?

Then I felt a hand on my forehead. I'd always been able to feel when I was touched; a mixed blessing. But this touch was different; it somehow *penetrated* into my mind. As the touch continued, I felt my body begin to awaken. Soon, my eyes began to focus and I could control them. Next, I tried to move my tongue and found that I could.

"Free!" It was difficult but I got the word out.

Before long, I was seeing and talking. Free introduced me to the two most beautiful men I have ever seen. Scotty and Kirk were like knights on white chargers come to rescue me even though it was actually Spock who was bridging the 'gap' between my brain and body. And Spock couldn't continue long. The strain of helping me was difficult for him. So I reluctantly said goodbye, confident that they would find a more permanent solution.

Of course, I remained aware while they worked out the solution. Spock would send for an 'orphan brain' from his home planet and it would be applied to my body. It would be an experiment but everyone had great hopes for it so I did too.

When the orphan brain was applied to my back, I regained control of my body almost immediately. Of course, my muscles hadn't been used for twenty-four years so I needed extensive therapy and re-training but I was actually on the mend!

A few weeks later, I walked out the door of that nursing home a free woman.

Free and Kirk opened their door to me. At first, it was their spare room and I was happy just to be able to rest in a bed by myself. But now sleeping alone while knowing they were together just a short distance away was difficult for me. I suppose my body was awakening in more ways than one.

So one day, while Kirk was at one of his many appointments, having a prosthesis fitted for his missing right hand, I approached Free.

"Sis, remember how we used to play together?"

"I sure do. I miss that."

"I miss it too. It's been a long time. Do you do stuff like that now?"

"You mean with women?"

"Yeah."

"It hasn't happened yet but I discussed it with Kirk and he's OK with it. I told him about the things we used to do and it really got him hot."

"So we could fool around in front of him?"

"We could, but why not both of us fool around WITH him?"

"You'd share him with me?"

"Of course. We shared Paul and all those guys in the gang didn't we?"

"But Kirk is special to you."

"And you're special to me, too."

"OK, but how should we do this?"

"When Kirk gets home, you pretend to be me and meet him at the door. He'll kiss you, thinking you're me. By the time he finds out the truth, he'll be too turned on to back out."

"Now I'm getting all trembly and excited. I kissed Spock and that cute Doctor Johnson on the cheek but I haven't seriously even kissed anybody in twenty-four years."

"And when we're alone, Kirk is a very aggressive kisser. He also does a lot of groping so you should be prepared for that. Maybe I should kiss and grope you the way he does me then when you get used to that, you kiss and grope me that way and I'll teach you how I respond."

So for the next hour or so, we 'practiced' kissing and groping.

"Oh, Free. Maybe a better plan would be for Kirk to just find us in bed."

"But we don't want to be too exhausted to have fun with him. Trust me, he's worth the wait."

So when Kirk came home, it was to a pair of very horny women. It was all I could do not to drag him directly to bed. I managed to play my part, though, and he was thoroughly confused. He only put up token resistance and the night was heaven. I was and I still am a little bit in love with Kirk but I don't want to take him away from my sister.

But the incident convinced me that I needed a man of my own. The only man available was Scotty and he suited me perfectly. Not only is he great looking, he has a quirky sense of humor that might not appeal to everyone but I love it. He's by far the most intelligent person I've ever met and he fits right in to the swinging lifestyle I wanted to live. To top it all off, he's the wealthiest Human to ever exist. Money isn't terribly important to me but it's nice to know that we'll never be living on the street. Our personalities just seem to 'mesh' in all the right places.

I'm not going to rehash all the adventures Kirk already described in his journals. His series of books entitled Star Tricks are available and I strongly recommend them.

More recently, while the Federation fleet, assisted by the Carmalan fleet from the M-33 galaxy, was dealing with the outlaw fleet controlled by the renegade male Arachna named Marvin, The Carmalans had mentally 'downloaded' a lot of information about Arachna science. The science used by the Arachna is indistinguishable from magic to most people. It has always failed to work for anyone other than the Arachna despite their efforts to teach it to others.

The Carmalans discovered that the key to using Arachna science was an inborn psionic ability. While the Carmalans have psionic ability, their mental makeup does not allow them to successfully use Arachnan science. The psionic ability that I gained with my grafted Vulcan brain made me a perfect candidate to receive the downloaded Arachna science.

Shortly after the Carmalan representative aboard the *Enterprise* had uploaded the Arachna science into my mind, we were attacked by a supposedly captive ship that had escaped. I was able to use Arachna science to defend the *Enterprise*, destroying the escaped ship.

I am not a violent person and I still have nightmares about taking all those lives.

96

However, I remind myself that if I hadn't done it, the *Enterprise* and nearly everyone I know and love would have been killed.

An Arachna volunteer, RaeLyn, has moved to the *Enterprise* for the time being and she is helping me learn the fine points of Arachna science. Of course, some of it is entirely within the mind but other parts involve chemical and physical manipulation. Those parts will take a lot of study.

Kirk has let me read the portion of his book that is already written. I can only add my heartfelt endorsement of Kirk James. The man is absolutely the best thing that ever happened to the Milky Way galaxy and I do hope he will consent to be Galactic Emperor. I'm certain that the vast majority of the galactic population will want this too.

Charlotte Christine Montgomery

Note: Well, I should have expected that.

Kirk

CHAPTER IX: LinDo

Hello, you probably don't remember me from Admiral James's journals because I was only mentioned briefly in a minor role but he asked me to tell you about my home world.

In reading his published work, I see that he actually knows very little of my home world despite several visits there. I suppose that is to be expected; our society is very different from any other I have seen in my travels.

First and foremost is the fact that he has never seen a female Elidorian. That is not surprising because our females only very rarely appear in public and when they do, they cover their entire bodies in fabric. This is not due to the wishes of the males, it's a social necessity that the males would mostly like to see changed but it is so deeply ingrained in our society that I doubt it will ever change.

For many generations, we have maintained a computer network very similar to Earth's internet. Over the years, nearly all social interaction has taken place by computer. When a young male wishes to find a mate, he uses his computer. Once he locates a possible match, he must negotiate with her mother. If he clears that hurdle, he is allowed to visit her home but only under the supervision of her father or other adult male relative. He will never see or directly

99

interact with her mother; all communications to this point have been by text. If the young couple decides to mate, the father gets the singular honor of paying for a civil ceremony. Of course, this is not the extravaganza it is on Earth because no females will attend and the 'bride' must be hidden from view.

After the ceremony, neither parent will ever see their daughter again. They often will be in contact by text on the computer but protocol prevents video or voice. The young male mate is completely responsible for his 'bride' and would never consider asking his 'father-in-law' for anything.

Admiral James has also expressed some confusion regarding some of our physical attributes. For one thing: our luxuriant fur. Until the discovery of energy-gathering fields, our planet had a very cool climate. In response, our bodies developed the fur to keep us warm. We've had a much warmer environment for many generations but not nearly long enough to lose our fur.

Another thing is our large, pointed teeth. Our ancestors were predatory carnivores but their prey was exclusively one species of animal. Our scientists tell us that when the climate began to cool, that prey animal became extinct. Our ancestors were forced to eat vegetables or die. Now, our digestive systems have adapted so well that we are unable to digest animal protein in any form and must exist on strictly vegetables even though we retain the teeth of carnivores.

The last point I would like to address for Admiral James is our nasal appendages. All male Elidorians have a nasal appendage very similar to the trunk of an Earthly elephant but much smaller; the average being six to seven inches in Earthly measurement. Frankly, we have no use for them but scientists tell us they believe the appendages were much longer on our ancestors and were somehow used in mating. Ancient drawings depict great leaders with very long appendages. In modern times, they are more of a nuisance than anything else. The only use is while swimming; it makes breathing convenient.

I hope this brief summary will answer the questions of Admiral James and others. Admiral James is a hero to everyone on my world and all the people there wish him the very best in anything he wishes to do. All, of course, hope he will consent to be Galactic Emperor but that is, of course, his choice.

LinDo

Note: This is getting monotonous. Can't SOMEBODY say something bad about me?

Kirk James

CHAPTER X: T'prau

Greetings. My name is Technopraunicnorianiachoignialian but I would not expect most Humans to remember or pronounce that. I selected the Human-use name T'prau for that very reason.

I fear I must be brief as my beloved Spock has already told you much of the information I could have given you.

I was born on the planet now known as Vulcan at approximately the same time the celebrated American President Abraham Lincoln was born on Earth. Of course, we were as unaware of the birth of Mister Lincoln as Earth citizens were unaware of my birth. It was only when he became prominent in American politics that our explorers became aware of his existence.

And of course, my existence was unknown on Earth until the publishing of the journals of Admiral James.

From a very early age, I demonstrated an affinity for computer science. After completing my basic education, I attended the Academy of Science and obtained the equivalent of a Master of Arts degree in computer programming. Certainly in our language, the title is different but it amounts to the same thing.

With this education, I sought and obtained employment with a large medical practice.

I continued this employment for many years but after some time found myself restless and bored.

Many would have sought other employment or a mate. Instead, I chose to return to the Academy to study medicine. I had always enjoyed the academic life and was intrigued by the medical aspect of my job. I did not expect to actually practice medicine but felt a better understanding would be helpful.

During the course of this study, I accepted a temporary roommate. S'ponkavonvetchakinaian, as he was then known, was a bright young person, slightly younger that I, but I found him intellectually stimulating and we soon developed a strong friendship.

Of course, S'ponkavonvetchakinaian is now known as Spock and I will refer to him as such to avoid confusion.

From our first meeting, Spock and I felt a special bond formed of mutual admiration and respect. I particularly admired his keen mind and sharp wit. He always seemed to know the correct course of action is any situation. Of course, at that time our sexual organs were dormant so the attraction was merely intellectual but it was powerful.

Whenever I envisioned the future, I could not imagine it without Spock.

All my life, when I pictured myself mated, I always saw myself in the female role. When Spock and I began discussing becoming mates, I automatically assumed that I would become the female even though Spock had been the female half of a mated pair previously. This question had not been decided when Spock was forced to depart precipitously. While he was gone, I impulsively decided to proceed with the process of becoming female.

As I wanted to be the best female possible for Spock, I prevailed on some medically knowledgeable friends to administer hormone therapy in order to accentuate my transformation. The result was far more successful than any of us expected.

Most Vulcan females do not grow hair on their heads and their breasts are merely adequate for feeding infants. In fact, to all appearances, they are difficult to distinguish from males.

However, the hormone therapy has caused me to look much as a Human female does, with luxuriant hair, large breasts, and wide hips. Most Vulcan males do not find this attractive but Spock's long association with Humans has changed his perspective so we are both very pleased by my appearance.

Human males also seem to find me attractive. This is not a problem between Spock and me as we seem to be lacking the sexual jealousy that seems to be responsible for so many Human miseries. If one of us enjoys an encounter with another person, that does not in any way interfere with our relationship. No other woman or group of women can possibly 'use him up' and he will always return. In fact, I enjoy watching him perform with other women; I find it very stimulating. In return, he tells me that he feels the same way. He particularly enjoys watching me with other women, something I also enjoy.

Since I first learned of Earth and its inhabitants, I have been fascinated by the people and traditions, especially those from the North American political area known as the United States. After I began sharing Spock's quarters on the Enterprise, we discussed making our mating more formal than is usual for our people. We decided on a ceremony common in the United States and Admiral James was gracious enough to acquiesce. The entire ship's company joined in the festivities and it was a memorable occasion. Admiral James describes it well in his first collection of journals, published as Star Tricks, so I will not embellish it here.

Our marriage has been ideal, if not one everyone would want. We do not 'cleave to each other' as tradition says we should. We frequently share the pleasures of others and do so with the full knowledge and often the encouragement of each other. But we see nothing wrong in this and enjoy it. If we ever cease to enjoy it, we will stop. Free and Kirk, Easy and Scotty, and several other of our friends have similar marriage arrangements; they also find contentment and fulfillment in this manner.

Apart from sex, Spock and I share a wonderful relationship on an intellectual level. We share many interests such as entertainment and food. We also each have our own interests: My primary fields of study have always been computer science and medicine while Spock enjoys structural engineering and mathematics. We spend many pleasurable evenings studying together quietly. Because we each know enough about the other's interests, we are able to have many interesting discussions encompassing varying subjects.

We both fully expect our marriage to endure throughout our remaining lives and although our ages may sound advanced to Humans, we are only considered 'middle aged' among our own people.

Admiral James had allowed me to read the previous entries in this volume and I wish to add my endorsement to the others. He is the ideal and only logical candidate to become Galactic Emperor. He is revered and trusted by nearly every civilized being in the galaxy and I can name no other entity who can match that qualification.

Technopraunicnorianiachoignialian

(T'prau)

You, too, huh? K. M. J.

CHAPTER XI: The Monty Car

No, of course the Monty Car can do many wonderful things but it can't speak or write. I prevailed on Scotty to write a chapter describing the development of the Monty Car because it was the source of his wealth and also essentially the 'ancestor' of the *Enterprise* and many other of his marvelous developments.

K. M. J.

Hello. Like the proverbial bad penny, I'm back. Kirk wants me to talk about the beginnings of the Monty Car.

Kirk has already described the discovery of the field that has been dubbed the Montgomery Field. When the table suddenly shot against the wall, I noticed that it stopped a few inches short of actually striking the wall. Kirk's coffee, which was sitting there at the edge of the table, didn't spill or even ripple. None of the various electronic components which were lying loose on the table were disturbed even slightly despite the very abrupt movement of the table. When I examined the situation closely, I noticed that the legs of the table were approximately two inches above the floor; the table appeared to be 'floating' in mid-air.

My attempts to reach the bread-board circuit were at first defeated by extremely firm resistance. But I found that slow persistent pressure would penetrate and I was eventually able to reach in to turn off the field.

This began the first of many long nights of study and experiment. Over time, I learned that I could shape and modify the field by controlling voltages and the precise application of current. And after the field was started by a small electrical charge, it needed no further outside power; in fact, it had more energy that it needed. I learned that I could use a field to power other electrical equipment. After a time, I cancelled electrical service to my home, powering everything with a relatively weak field; you could easily walk through it but it absorbed more power than I needed for all my electrical needs.

I could probably have become wealthy with just this application but to me it was merely a 'side issue'. As related earlier, my parents were killed in an automobile accident when I was twelve years old and it left me with a distrust of automobiles. Certainly I drove and rode in cars but I was never comfortable. I was very impressed that despite the velocity of the table, there was no impact when it reached the wall. Could this be developed into a safe form of transportation?

My experiments taught me that the field could be controlled very simply by a computer. I spent a lot of time developing computer programs designed for just this purpose.

My first experimental vehicle was a simple platform with a seat, a control console, and a safety 'cage' that I sincerely hoped was unnecessary. Loading it into a borrowed pickup truck, Kirk and I hauled it out of town to a large empty farm field.

When I activated the field, the platform rose a few inches from the ground and 'hovered'. Moving the joystick slightly forward caused the platform to take off at an incredible rate of speed; much faster than I expected. Before I could react, I had run from the edge of the field into a stand of trees.

When the foremost part of the field encountered a tree, the platform stopped instantly. But throughout all this, I had felt no acceleration or deceleration. I felt no impact and the only injury was to my nerves.

"Are you okay, Scott?" Kirk had jogged over while I was collecting myself.

"I guess so. I believe this thing needs some adjustment."

"We don't need an ambulance?"

"Nope. Even the platform is undamaged. I think we're on to something; it just needs fine-tuning."

After that, I learned to adjust the current to the directional control. Once I had an 'accelerator', the platform proved very easy to drive.

My next refinement was to the vertical control. I learned that the platform could go up and down just as easily as forward, back, left, and right. Once in the sky and away from most obstacles, I could increase the velocity. The field protected me from the wind so one day I decided to see what it would do. I took 'er up to a respectable altitude and moved at a sedate speed quite some distance from what we had come to think of as our testing ground. Turning around, I headed back, moving the 'throttle' slowly further forward than I ever had before.

"Scotty! Slow down!" We had a radio setup and Kirk sounded panicked so I quickly pulled back on the throttle.

"What's wrong, Kirk?"

"I bet you were breaking windows all over town."

"How could I be breaking windows?"

"With that sonic boom; you were breaking the sound barrier."

I had been nowhere near the maximum travel on the throttle. If I was ever going to make this a commercial success, it may need some artificial restriction; we couldn't have everyone's family car causing sonic booms.

I eventually learned to make the field into a mile-long, narrow 'needle', very streamlined. With this configuration, a car can get up to Mach Five without causing a sonic boom. The field elongates as the car gains speed, not only to eliminate booms, but to gently move small objects from the car's path. In the case of larger obstacles, the car is deflected and the onboard computer automatically modifies the course.

But at first, it was 'by guess and by gosh'. Nothing like this had ever been done before and I had to work out each step as I went. My little collision with the trees had taught me to slightly elongate and taper the field. This proved to have an unexpected benefit:

One day, I was 'hot-rodding' around our test field. I thought Kirk had gone into town to pick up something for our lunch so I wasn't watching for him. When he suddenly stepped into view, directly in my path, I couldn't react quickly enough.

Certain that I'd killed my best friend; I quickly stopped and hopped from my vehicle only to find Kirk standing to the side, completely unhurt and only slightly shaken.

"What happened?"

"When you almost hit me, I was suddenly just moved to the side. It didn't hurt and the car never came close to me. I found myself standing several feet away but not injured."

I didn't have any way to measure velocity in the car yet but I estimated that I had been traveling at least one hundred miles per hour. If I had been driving a conventional gasoline car, Kirk would certainly have been killed.

This was a safety feature I hadn't expected. I certainly wanted to protect drivers and passengers but somehow, pedestrians would be safer too.

To test a theory (and because Kirk likes playing with toys anyway), I 'buzzed' a radio-controlled model airplane at near-sonic speed. The airplane was gently moved to the side but its flight was not disrupted. My vehicle was even safer than I had imagined.

The next test would have to wait until I could build another vehicle. I wanted to see what would happen if two of these vehicles ran into each other. Yes, Kirk and I were going to become 'crash-test dummies'.

Well, all we could get them to do was deflect their courses. On one rare occasion, we actually got them to strike so 'squarely' that both came to a sudden halt. But even though both of us had been moving at a respectable velocity, there was no violence to us or our vehicles. We were both wearing seat belts but they were not needed. Kirk's ever-present coffee didn't even spill.

"I think you're onto something here, Scotty."

"Yeah, but what do I do with it?"

"Well, the vehicle is the safest thing to ever move anybody and it doesn't even use fuel. It has to have a commercial use."

"Exactly. But how do I get it on the market? You know the oil companies and the auto industry are going to hate it. And it'll need money to develop."

"Well, between us, we have hundreds of dollars. But we're going to need a lot more than that. Some legal and political muscle is certain to be needed too."

"I'll just have to call in a marker."

"I didn't know you had any markers that large."

"When you started talking about legal and political muscle, you made me think of a guy my company did some work for a few months ago. They sent me to his place to custom design and install some pretty advanced electronics."

"I remember. You were gone for about a month."

"That's the job. I wasn't really sworn to secrecy but they asked me not to talk much about it. Well, the client was Robert van Gelder."

"THE Robert van Gelder?"

"Himself. And he was very impressed with my work. Besides a very large under-the-table tip, he told me if he could ever do anything for me, to give him a call."

"I believe that would be a good call to make. I hope you didn't throw away his number."

I have his private number at home, under lock and key."

"Before you call him, we should work out a demonstration that will show off what these things can do."

So we began finding out exactly what they could do. We learned that the field could easily become air-tight. We learned that if the car was turned upside-down, the 'floor' of the vehicle still felt like 'down' to the occupant. This made me realize that the field could be used to manipulate gravity. I filed that away for future investigation.

In all, riding in or driving one of these cars felt exactly like sitting still; you could only tell you were moving by visual references.

"But should we just show him a sheet of plywood with a seat and a control box?"

"I had an idea about that. Remember that 'Future Car' Jake's Auto Body made out of fiberglass for last year's Homecoming Parade?"

"Yeah, that was pretty impressive-looking."

"Jake says he's tired of it taking up room in his shop and he'll sell it cheap. All we need to do is put in a decent interior and the control electronics."

"It'll need a paint job, too."

"I bet we can get a deal from Jake."

So we bought the 'Future Car' from Jake and began transforming the interior. Fortunately, Jake had put in a flashy interior complete with all kinds of fake gadgets. We only needed to replace them with real instruments. The car was mostly fiberglass but had a minimal tubular steel frame to keep it fairly rigid but it was nowhere near automotive quality. This didn't bother us because we didn't expect it to be subjected to any stress.

The car only had two fancy-looking bucket seats and they weren't especially comfortable but looked great.

117

I decided that the steering wheel could go along with the pedals. In their place was a small desk with a keyboard and joystick along with a touchpad in place of the traditional mouse. I decided we wouldn't want a driver looking for a dropped mouse while operating a vehicle; the touchpad could be mounted solidly. Another innovation was a control wheel for the speed range control; at the lowest setting, the vehicle would just 'creep' while if you dialed it up, it really moved.

In the center of the dashboard, Jake had installed a fake computer screen. I replaced that with a real laptop. Since it was there, I decided to have it do something. Installing GPS software, I managed to convince the computer to ignore streets once the car was airborne. You could punch in an address, raise the car above nearby obstacles, and the car would fly you directly and quickly to your destination. After that, you had to 'land' the car manually. We managed to sneak home after dark that way a couple times. The GPS 'knew' addresses all over North America but we didn't dare try any road trips at that point.

Of course the car wasn't legal on the street, on the highway, or in the air. It didn't qualify as a motor vehicle or as an airplane and certainly didn't meet anybody's safety regulations. It didn't have lights, brakes, or even an engine. If it was ever going to be legal to operate, it would need to be a whole new class of vehicle.

****

RIIIIIIIIIIIIIING

"Hello?"

"Mister van Gelder?"

"Yes."

"I can't believe you answer your own phone."

"Well, it's my phone."

"I suppose it is. My name is Scott Montgomery. My company 'loaned' me to your company a few months ago and I wound up doing some work in your home. Do you remember me?"

"I certainly do! You solved a ton of problems, both for my company and in my home. Those alleged 'experts' on my payroll had no idea what they were doing. Did you reconsider that job offer I made you?"

"Not exactly, Sir. But I'm thinking of a private enterprise venture and I really could use your help. There's something you need to see. A description just won't do it justice. Can you send a representative to my proving ground here in east central Iowa?"

"I can do better than that; I'm tired of just sitting around board rooms. I'll come myself. When can you be ready?"

"My brother and I have been preparing a demonstration but didn't expect you to come personally. Give us a couple more days. How does Thursday afternoon sound?"

"I have nothing on my agenda. Give me the location and I'll be there."

Robert van Gelder was extremely wealthy and was famous for hating Big Oil. He had sworn to 'take down' several of the major petroleum interests but had never found the opportunity to do so. Also, his beloved wife and children had been killed in an automobile accident involving a drunken driver. He was not directly involved in politics but had strong political connections at the congressional level.

Now that van Gelder was actually coming, Kirk and I started sweating every detail of our presentation. Should we show him this or do that? Would this impress him or scare him? If we do this, will it make a good impression? And we still didn't even know exactly what the car was capable of doing.

Fortunately, I had plenty of vacation time available from my job. Kirk was able to set his own hours so we spent the next few days figuring out exactly what to show our visitor.

****

Mister van Gelder arrived early Thursday afternoon in a stretch limo accompanied by his attorney, Mark Detlie, and his business manager, Bill DeNato along with a recording secretary and a photographer.

"I hope you don't mind that I brought my entourage but I understood that you wanted to discuss business. These people are important for that purpose."

"That's no problem, Sir. Indeed we hope to talk business but first we want to show you what we have. After that, you can decide if you want to be involved with it. All we ask is that if you decide not to become involved, you not discuss what you are about to see with anyone. A security leak could be disastrous for us.

"That sounds like a fair request. I agree and extend the agreement to the people who work for me; if they couldn't be trusted, they wouldn't work for me."

We had been fortunate enough to be presented with a beautiful Iowa spring day. Kirk and I had borrowed a friend's pickup truck and hauled six easy chairs to the edge of the field in order to accommodate our visitors. A couple of beach umbrellas for shade and a cooler of assorted beverages completed our VIP seating.

Once everyone was comfortable, I began my presentation.

"Mister van Gelder, distinguished visitors, this all began when I was experimenting with generating a force field. I succeeded far beyond my expectations. The field I discovered

121

is not only a force field, it absorbs energy from an unknown source, becoming self-powering and even has more power than it needs. The field can also move itself and anything within itself at a great and controllable velocity. Somehow, inertia is negated within the field. If the field and enclosed objects strike anything, they stop instantly with no damage or violence to the stricken object or the objects inside the field. The field has many other interesting properties and we are still exploring them. Over there, (I indicated our two platforms with seats and control boxes.) are our two test vehicles. We would like to demonstrate some of the things they can do. Bear in mind that they use no fuel of any kind and produce absolutely no pollution."

Kirk and I each boarded a test vehicle and we proceeded to play a short game of 'bumper cars'. Of course, we were unable to even get the cars to make contact. After that, I parked mine and Kirk drove to the far side of the field while I approached our audience.

"Folks, a little further away you can see a group of assorted obstacles placed at random in the field. Kirk will drive back through the center of those obstacles at high speed making no attempt to avoid them. We'd like you to observe what happens."

We had placed oil drums, orange traffic cones, and a couple of chairs out in the field. Several of them held fragile pieces of glasswork.

122

Kirk came barreling back through the center of the obstacles and the field moved them all gently to the side well in advance of his arrival. None of the obstacles was upset or any of the glasswork broken. I then 'accidentally' wandered onto the test area as Kirk came back for a second run. Just like the other obstacles, I was moved gently to the side.

"Folks, what we have is a vehicle that doesn't use fuel, doesn't pollute, and is totally incapable of harming anyone, either inside or outside of itself."

Van Gelder was sitting there, stunned. "And this isn't some kind of trick?"

"No trick, Sir. We'd like to produce and market these but of course we'll need legal and financial backing. That's why I contacted you."

"Are these things difficult to operate?"

"Not difficult at all, Sir. In fact, we have another one we haven't shown you yet and we'd like to invite you to drive it."

"I'd probably wreck it and break my fool neck."

"We thought you might have that reaction." I gave Kirk the 'thumbs up'

Kirk took his test vehicle high into the air, turned around, and began a 'power dive' directly at the ground.

123

"You'll notice that he isn't wearing a safety belt."

"My God, he'll be killed!"

"Just watch."

Kirk approached the ground at well over two hundred miles per hour. But at about fifteen feet above the ground, his vehicle came to an abrupt halt and just hung there. He wasn't even shifted in his seat. After a few moments, he leveled his vehicle then landed.

"Mister van Gelder, that was just to demonstrate that it's totally impossible to hurt yourself or anyone else with one of these vehicles. Even a drunk driver may be an annoyance but he is no longer a threat to others."

I could see the pain cross his face but my point struck home. If these vehicles came into common use, no one else would lose their family to drunk drivers the way he had.

"I guess I should try this vehicle."

"Right over here, Sir."

"Please call me Bob; I believe we're going to be in business together for quite some time."

"Okay, Bob. We have a nicer vehicle we were saving for this moment."

I pulled the canvas tarp from the Future Car we had purchased from Jake's Auto Body and fixed up. After we got finished with the interior, we took it back to Jake who did wonders with the paint job. It was now a bright metallic blue with silver accents. After the paint was well set, it had received several coats of paste wax and it now fairly gleamed in the bright Iowa sun.

"It's beautiful!"

"It's really only a concept car. I actually visualize a family vehicle as something more like a minivan but this was more fun."

"Why does it have wheels?"

"We got the car already built and converted it. Besides that, if the frame was resting on the ground, it would be difficult to enter and exit. A vehicle designed from the beginning to use the field would have a different arrangement."

"And you say these cars don't use oil?"

"The only petroleum in this entire vehicle was used to lubricate the door hinges. And if necessary, hinges can be designed to operate nicely without oil."

"Well, let's give it a try."

Once inside, he was confused by the lack of pedals or a steering wheel.

"Okay, the large joystick controls direction. Push forward to go forward, pull back to move backward, etc. Twisting the joystick controls the way the nose of the vehicle is facing. That takes a little practice but it's easier than it sounds. The small joystick next to the big one controls the attitude of the vehicle; if you push it forward while in the air, the vehicle's nose will tilt down. Keep it forward and the vehicle turns a summersault. Left, right, and backwards do the same in the other directions. To your left is the speed control or 'throttle'. It's set below 'one' right now and I suggest you leave it there until you get the feel of the vehicle. Once you get used to it, you can add speed. The oversized thumbwheel beside that controls altitude. Those are the only controls you need for local driving. Any other controls are for long-distance navigation and I hope eventually to have that mostly computerized."

"Just how fast will this thing go?"

"I haven't found out yet. I had it up to slightly over seven hundred miles per hour but it could have gone much faster."

"So you're proposing a family car capable of supersonic flight?"

"Remember, there will be no mid-air collisions or other accidents. But it may still be necessary to have the computer automatically take over above a certain speed or limit the maximum speed. It will depend on what the lawmakers will allow."

126

"I have some ideas about how to handle the lawmakers. Let's try the car and I'll discuss the ideas with Mark to be sure we won't get into trouble trying them."

"All right. Start by entering the password to the main computer."

"What's the password?"

"I was afraid you might need some ego-stroking so the password is capital "R", lower case "v", and capital "G"."

"My initials! Well, I'm not likely to forget that."

After he entered the three letters, the driver's instruments illuminated.

"Now, you simply move the altitude control to the first click to raise the car above the ground. After that, just practice moving around with the joystick."

It was only a few minutes before he was driving confidently around the farm field. He could easily handle the car, even at relatively high velocity.

"If you'd like to try flying it, you can but you should be aware that as long as we're on private property, we're ok but this vehicle isn't legal on a public road or in the air."

"Yeah, I'm a licensed pilot, too, but I just can't resist taking 'er up. There's very little chance of getting caught here. And how many police aircraft can fly as fast as this car?"

"They can't shoot us down, either; the field becomes very tough to penetrate as our velocity increases. I doubt a bullet or missile could touch us."

"So we're bulletproof too? This thing just gets better and better."

"I'm still experimenting with the field but I believe I can make even a stationary field extremely tough when wanted. I suspect that a properly configured field would be proof against even a nuclear weapon."

"So I could put a field over my home and never worry about security?"

"I believe that would be relatively simple. The field would be self-powering so burglars or attackers couldn't disrupt your power. You could have a securely coded remote control to operate the field while away from home."

"Like many wealthy, influential men, I tend to collect enemies and security threats. When my family was living, I had to employ a small army just to ensure their safety. Even now, my driver doubles as a bodyguard."

"I noticed a complex alarm system in your home when I was there. I'm not an expert

128

on alarm systems but as an electronics engineer; I could see several weaknesses in the system."

"And even the best security guards can be bribed or tricked. I hate to sound paranoid but it's hard to know whom to trust these days."

"I haven't really designed a field as a home security system but it shouldn't be difficult to do."

"If you do that, I can promise you that we'll get your car on the market as quickly as possible. Not only will it save countless lives, it'll kill the oil companies."

"It will also adversely affect people like highway workers, sign painters, traffic cops, even fast food employees. In fact, it will turn the entire planet's economy on its ear."

"Well, the current economy is nothing to brag about. Let's shake things up and let them seek a new level. I'd sure like to see those oil execs on the bottom of the heap for a change."

While this conversation was taking place, we had climbed to five thousand feet and were well on our way to Chicago at six hundred miles per hour.

"As much as I'd like to, we probably shouldn't enter Chicago's airspace. We're no danger to aircraft but Chicago Center won't know that and we'd cause a lot of panic."

"And at this speed, they have to know we're not some farmer in a Piper Cub."

"I guess we should go back before too many people get a close look at this car. It needs to be kept a secret until we're ready to spring it on the public."

"This goes against common logic but just turn the joystick until the nose is pointing back in the direction of Iowa. Then, push forward. The lack of inertia means we won't even notice the change in direction."

"Hey! That was really something! Our relative change in velocity had to be nearly one thousand miles per hour and I didn't even feel it. Now, how do I find your proving ground?"

"Go to the navigation computer, call up the GPS menu, and select 'Home'."

With the computer in command, we could relax and enjoy the scenery on the trip back.

*** DING!***

"That means we're over our destination. I haven't 'taught' the car to land yet so it will just hover here until you take it down."

By now, Bob had a feel for operating the car. He simply dialed the altitude down until we were about ten feet above the ground, circled to be sure our intended landing area was clear, and then settled right back onto the spot where he boarded the car.

****

Over the course of the next couple of years, Bob hired me away from the engineering firm. I'm sure some of the 'button counters' in his accounting department wondered why an employee who lived in Iowa and never even punched a time clock was drawing such a large paycheck with benefits along with a big operational budget that wasn't itemized. Bob just told them to mind their own business. Of course, such things WERE their business but they had learned not to question Bob.

Of course I needed an assistant and who else was available but Kirk M. James? With a hefty salary and benefits, of course.

On the advice of the attorneys Bob retained for the project, we kept everything as hush-hush as possible; if the oil companies found out about our project too early, they could conceivably resort to drastic measures to stop us. The patent attorney team was obtaining patents for as many applications of the field as we could possibly dream of. When I had time to think about it, my dream was finally 'on track' but most of the time, I was just too busy.

Bob's political connections got us an audience with some very highly placed people in the Congressional Transportation Committee. By this time, Kirk and I had a couple of

131

prototype cars that looked a lot like minivans without wheels but certainly weren't made to meet current highway safety standards or airworthiness directives. We had a routine worked out to demonstrate the capabilities of the vehicles that was similar to the one we had shown Bob; it was a little more polished but essentially the same. One innovation I especially liked was a live webcam watching a goldfish bowl resting on a table in one of the vehicles while the vehicle was performing aerobatics. The fish swam undisturbed. That demonstration finished with the vehicle ramming a brick wall at two hundred miles per hour. The politicos were invited to visit the fish after that. Of course they were still undisturbed.

After that, the Transportation Committee felt that this new type of vehicle should be approved for public use. They started drafting bills to classify the vehicle as an 'all-purpose safety vehicle' and the requirements made sure that no other form of powering such a vehicle could qualify for the class.

"Bob, we never did actually discuss your cut of my income from all of this."

"Don't worry. Sure, I'm investing a lot of money in this but when this storm breaks, it'll totally kill the oil companies. Besides that, I'll know when it's going to happen. With the proper stock preparation, I stand to at least double my money."

"So you're not just being a 'nice guy'."

132

"Scott, I like you and I'm happy to help you out but I'm putting a lot of money into this. I wouldn't do that unless there was something in it for me. The biggest thing that convinced me was the fact that these vehicles will stop the bloodbath on the highways. That's worth any amount of money to me after losing my family. Nobody should ever have to deal with the pain I suffered."

In an amazingly short time, Monty cars were everywhere. Gasoline-powered cars were going the way of the dinosaur and the world's economy was experiencing a major re-adjustment. Not only was the price of oil at an all-time low, most automobile-related industry was going belly-up. This included some things you might not think about at first: motels, fast food restaurants, highway maintenance, traffic cops, and many more. Even companies manufacturing and selling supplies for those professions were feeling the pinch.

I felt responsible for putting all those people out of work and decided I should do something about it.

My primary goal most of my life had been to go to space. Now, I had what I believed could be a perfect star drive and I had enough money and power to do anything I wanted.

I decided to build a starship.

So I had my lawyers start buying up defunct automobile manufacturing plants along with steel mills and other assorted facilities. Skilled labor was sitting around just begging for work so I hired them; first to get the factories back in operation then to await orders for starship sub-assemblies.

In the mean time, I had the finest team of architects and engineers working on plans for the ship. I had a general shape in mind but it was up to them to make it work. And I offered bonuses for rapid results. Once again, I proved the old adage that 'money talks'. Never mind what walks.

"But Scotty, you don't even know if this drive will work in space."

"Well, why don't we take a little trip to find out?"

"Surely you can't be serious."

"I am serious. And don't call me Shirley."

"You watch too many old movies, Scotty."

"Leslie Nielson was one of my heroes."

"Back to the original discussion: what about this space trip?"

"We'll just modify an existing vehicle and take a short trip in outer space. No big deal."

"How much of a 'short trip'?"

134

"Like I said, no big deal; the moon."

"THE MOON????"

"It's been done before."

"Yeah, by NASA, after many years of experiments, testing, dry runs, and practice missions."

"Right, they did all the hard work for us."

"So you want to go to the moon in a tricked –out Monty car?"

"I want to be more comfortable than that. Let's use a bigger vehicle."

"What do you have in mind?"

"I think you have the perfect space vehicle in your back yard."

"The TITANIC????"

The Titanic was an ancient motor home that had been sitting in Kirk's back yard forever and a day. The engine hadn't run in years but he'd converted the body into sort-of a guest house. The wheels were still present but I doubt the tires would support the weight of the chassis. Well-hidden cinder blocks did that for them. The original twelve volt electrical system had long ago stopped functioning so Kirk and I had re-wired the whole unit with standard household circuitry along with a dynamite sound system.

"The Titanic is as good as anything else and it's comfortable."

"But it can't possibly be airtight."

"It doesn't need to be. I can put an airtight field closely around the Titanic then have a couple other fields further out for protection along with another field to move the whole shebang."

"You really think you can make this work?"

"If I didn't think it would work, I wouldn't risk my neck"

"If we're going into space in that motor home, we'll have to change its name. The last voyage of the *Titanic* was less than successful."

By now, there was no law against moving anything through public airspace as long as it was enclosed in a Montgomery field. We moved the motor home to a body shop where the frame we strengthened then the body was patched and painted. Without telling Kirk, I had them give our new 'spaceship' a racy, futuristic, paint job along with a new name across the front and along both sides.

"S. S. Andre Norton?"

"She was always one of my favorite writers 'way back when. I didn't even realize at the time that she was a woman but she sure could write. I now know that at the time, science

136

fiction was very much a 'man's game' and she was fighting the odds just to be accepted. I considered her right up there with Heinlein and Asimov."

"I'm not questioning naming the ship after such a great writer; what does the S. S. stand for?"

"Star Ship; what else?"

"You're not suggesting a trip to the stars in this, are you?"

"Naw. It doesn't carry enough provisions. And I don't have the asterogation computers I'd need to leave the solar system. Besides that, I'm waiting for the big ship to be finished."

"Whew. You had me worried for a minute."

"I've decided to assemble the ground crew. We'll need them when we launch the big ship and this little jaunt will be good practice for them."

"What will they do?"

"Essentially just keep in touch with us. By the time we launch the big ship, I hope to have a shuttle system operational so they can keep us supplied with consumables and possibly even personnel as needed. That will all depend on the beacon I'm developing and want to test on this trip."

"How are you going to test it?"

"I have a little robot designed to 'home' on a beacon that will be activated on Earth. We'll go to the far side of the moon and launch it. If successful, the robot will follow the beacon all the way back to Earth without colliding with anything. I'm setting it for maximum acceleration until it reaches atmosphere then reducing to mach five. I want to time it on its flight."

"So we're going straight to the far side of the moon?"

"That's not what I had in mind. While we're in the neighborhood, so to speak, I'd like to visit Tranquility Base."

"Now we're playing from the same sheet of music. There's a very famous golf ball I've always wanted to retrieve."

"But Kirk, we don't know which way he hit it or how far he hit it. Even if we knew the approximate area, that's a very rough surface. Even if we can find it, do we have the right to take it?"

"You're right, Scotty. I guess I'll just have to settle for my own moon rock collection."

"We can do that but you'll have to reach out through the field with long grabbers. Exposing even a small area of skin to hard

138

vacuum could be fatal and we don't have spacesuits."

'Is vacuum that dangerous?"

"Let me put it this way: did you ever give a girl a 'hickey'?"

"Well, yeah."

"Did you ever get carried away, suck too hard, and draw blood?"

"A time or two."

"Well, the vacuum on the moon or in outer space is much more intense than anything you can create with your mouth. And it will be applied to any skin exposed to it. A single finger stuck outside the field will begin bleeding through every pore and you could lose a lot of blood in a hurry. If a large part of your body is exposed, you experience what is known as explosive decompression. That's a fast and messy way to die."

"Remind me to pack some very good tongs for rock collecting."

I was actually exaggerating a touch for Kirk's benefit. There are documented cases of people surviving exposure to hard vacuum but I didn't want him taking any chances.

For our 'ground crew', I assembled specialists in communications and as many other specialties as I thought we might possibly need.

139

Because I intended to keep this staff on the payroll after the launch of the starship, I decided to give them a rank structure. And I couldn't think of anything 'ranker' than the U. S. Army.

I arbitrarily decided that the person in charge was a Lieutenant General with three Major Generals under him or her in charge of the major departments. Various other high ranks held positions of importance under them. In this manner, there was no question about who was in charge of what. The entire organization was dubbed Star Fleet Command after my beloved Star Trek. I know, such an organization wasn't necessary for this little moon trip but I was looking to the future when I hoped to have several star ships operating. I was still trying to employ as many people as possible anyway without simply throwing away money.

Star Fleet Command was as organized as possible; the S. S. *Andre Norton* was provisioned and as well-equipped as I could manage. Kirk had been briefed as much as possible although I'm not sure he retained much. I expected to do most of the 'driving' anyway but I planned to teach him after I figured it out myself.

It was time to set a launch date.

"Six AM Tomorrow???? Why does everything need to begin at the crack of dawn?" Kirk was only half-joking.

"Come to think of it, there's no real reason, other than getting a full day's work from the ground crew. We don't have or need a 'launch window' and the moon isn't going very far. What time tomorrow suits you?"

"How about right after lunch?"

"Works for me."

We had based Star Fleet Command on a large tract of land just outside Iowa City, Iowa. That may seem a strange location after most space launches originating from Florida but our home is in Iowa and this was convenient for us.

Kirk and I flew the *Andre Norton* to Star Fleet spaceport the night before launch. There's actually no reason we couldn't have launched from Kirk's back yard but this would look better for the paparazzi.

As requested, Star Fleet personnel had really dressed up the launch area. It actually looked as if something important was about to happen. There were several impressive buildings already in place with others under construction. In the near distance was the almost-completed campus of Star Fleet Academy.

Lieutenant General Roger Thornton would be acting as primary launch controller. Roger had actually been rather highly placed in the army before retiring so he was accustomed to giving orders and 'thinking on his feet'. I had great hopes for him as a mainstay of Star Fleet.

141

"Do you need a countdown?"

"We don't really need it but I suppose it's traditional and the press will expect it"

"I have a whole passel of small to mid-sized politicians clamoring to say a 'few words' prior to the launch."

"Anything but that!!!!!"

"Calm down, Kirk. Roger, tell the politicians that we failed to schedule time for speeches. We need to stick to our planned launch agenda. They can speak during breaks in the TV coverage."

For lunch, I had my favorite: meatloaf with mashed potatoes and gravy, washed down with chocolate milk and followed by copious amounts of strong black coffee. Kirk, having slept until almost launch time, had breakfast for lunch: pancakes and sausage followed by coffee.

Having fueled the 'inner men', we trooped valiantly aboard the *SS Andre Norton,* wearing our newly designed Star Fleet uniforms for the first time in public. These were similar to the uniforms worn on the original Star Trek program but not exact copies as I had some fear of copyright infringement difficulties.

One of the advantages of the field I discovered is that it can be used for communications. I had great hopes that it would be faster than light and that was one thing we hoped to prove on this flight.

Roger's voice came over the communicator and I knew it was also being amplified through loudspeakers to the assembled crowd.

"*SS Andre Norton,* This is Star Fleet Launch Control. We show you cleared for launch."

I spoke into my 'boom' mic, which was attached to my headset. "Control, This is *Andre Norton,* We show all systems and onboard personnel prepared for launch. You may begin countdown."

"Acknowledged, *Norton,* beginning countdown."

"T minus Ten"

"Nine"

"Eight"

"Seven"

"Six"

"Five"

"Four"

"Three"

"Two:

"One"

"Go!"

When he said 'Go', I punched the button and *Andre Norton* lifted smoothly from the ground and sailed quickly into the sky. It was exactly the same as watching your Aunt Matilda leave for church but everyone thought it was really something.

However, instead of assuming horizontal flight, we continued away from Earth.

"How high are we going?"

"Kirk, I thought you knew we were going to the moon."

"Oh. Which way is it?"

"I really have no idea."

"Then how are we going to get there?"

"Relax. I'm going up to orbital altitude and we'll sit there in one spot until the moon shows up. After that, I just drive directly at it."

"But NASA spent millions of dollars computing complex orbits to reach the moon."

"So I'm cheap. We don't need to worry about fuel consumption or orbits. We can use as much velocity as we need. So I'll simply follow line-of-sight directly to the moon."

"Somehow, that seems like cheating."

"There are no rules. NASA did it the only way they could while maintaining reasonable safety. Our safety is built-in."

"Speaking of safety, how high are we?"

"We're about ten miles from the surface of the Earth now. I've stopped acceleration and we're holding position over Star Fleet Headquarters while we wait for the moon to appear.

"Can't we go looking for it?"

"We could, but there's no hurry and this is the surest way to do this. This time of year and at this altitude, the moon should be popping over the horizon any minute."

"Just don't get confused and fly us into the sun." Sometimes Kirk can be a worry-wart.

"No chance of that; the sun is much further, larger, and hotter."

"And there's very little chance of finding a golf ball."

"Right." I hoped that settled that.

"Well, to misquote an old song: 'Here comes the moon'."

"Right on schedule." I was happy to have something to do; I aimed the nose of the *Norton* at the moonrise and applied acceleration.

"OK, we're finally on the way."

145

"How long will it take us to get there?"

"That's a very good question. It all depends on how much velocity I decide to use. And I have no reliable way of measuring velocity?"

"Why not? You can measure speed with the field probes."

"But speed relative to what? There's nothing directly behind us and Star Fleet Headquarters is rotating with the Earth. In fact, it's over the horizon by now. Any point on Earth would be receding from us at a considerable velocity even if we were standing still."

"How about a closing velocity with the moon?"

"I can do that. Hang on while I program it…..hmmmmmmmm… It seems that we're moving more quickly than I thought. Our present closing velocity is roughly one hundred fifty thousand miles per hour and we're slightly over forty-five thousand miles from the lunar surface."

"But we've only been in space for a little over an hour. The NASA missions took several days to reach the moon."

"They were using complex fuel-saving orbits. We're flying a straight line with constant acceleration. And when we get there, we won't need complicated braking maneuvers; we just slow to a stop above the lunar surface."

"What happens if you don't slow to a stop?"

"What happened when you drove that first test vehicle into the ground at two hundred miles per hour with no seat belt?"

"It came to a stop and I brought it around to a proper landing."

"This would be exactly the same but I want to slow and look things over on the way in. Now stop worrying."

■■■■■■■■■■■■■■■■■■■■■■■■■■■■■■■■■■■■

We had little trouble finding Tranquility Base; lunar maps are available on the internet and better ones can be purchased from NASA.

We got some excellent photos of the site of man's first lunar landing but we didn't touch a thing there; we didn't even allow *Andre Norton* to touch the lunar soil there. Some things are just sacred in our minds.

After filling a couple memory cards with photos, we moved several hundred miles away before actually landing the *Norton*. Spotting some likely-sized and interesting-looking rocks, Kirk began collecting through the open side door, using his long tongs and being

147

very careful not to allow any part of his body outside the field.

"I have a better moon rock collection than any museum on Earth."

"At a rough estimate, considering the cost of this trip, those rocks cost me about one million dollars per ounce."

"But I donated the ship!"

I grinned. "That's true, Old Buddy. You deserve those rocks."

"What do we do next?"

"We're not equipped for exploring so let's head for the dark side of the moon."

"Is it made of green cheese?"

"Nope; just rock and dust like this side."

"So I wasted my money on this long-handled cheese knife?"

"Tell me you didn't"

He just grinned. Kirk has a wicked sense of humor and can spend a lot of time setting up just the proper punch line. He really got me this time. He's really extremely intelligent but plays 'dumb' just forcing me to think and explain. Often in the process of explaining, I fine-tune my own thoughts. It's been this way since we were small boys and the roles work well for both of us. He's far less inept than his words make him sound.

Arriving at the far ('dark') side of Luna, we found that it wasn't any darker or significantly different from the more familiar side. The biggest difference being that accurate maps had been unavailable.

"What do we do now, Coach?"

"I don't know about you, Kirk, but I'm tired after driving somewhere around three hundred thousand miles. I think we'll go well around this side of the moon then set down for the 'night'."

"I thought we were going to take turns driving."

"I did too but it didn't occur to me til now and I'm too tired to teach you. We'll settle down for the night and continue after some rest."

"But we only have one full-sized bed."

"You sleep there; I'll reduce the gravity in the *Norton* to moon-normal, about one-sixth Earth gravity, and sleep here in this reclining seat."

"So at one-sixth gee, my one hundred seventy pounds will be a little less than thirty?"

:"Twenty-nine and change. I'm too tired to figure it and the gravity won't be exactly one-sixth."

"That should make for some comfortable sleeping conditions."

"I hope so. Some people experience a sensation of falling when exposed to reduced gravity. If you're uncomfortable, let me know. And watch that you don't bang your head on the ceiling."

So we settled down. I found that the reduced gravity made the reclining bucket seat as comfortable as any expensive mattress I'd ever felt.

Just as a precaution, I called Mission Control and asked them to wake us in eight hours. I then turned up the volume on the communicator, just to be sure.

****COCK A DOODLE DOO!!!****

Mission Control had decided to wake us by playing a recorded rooster crowing. Crude, but effective.

I had misjudged how high I had turned the volume on the communicator and the sudden loud rooster crowing startled me severely.

I thanked Mission Control, wryly, for the wake-up call and began thinking about breakfast.

These ruminations were soon interrupted by muffled cries for help from the bedroom at the rear of the *Andre Norton*.

150

Proceeding aft, I found Kirk. He had been even more startled than I by the rooster. Launching from the mattress in the low gravity and taking the blanket with him, he had become entangled in the ceiling fan.

"Are you going to help or laugh?"

"Probably laugh a while, then help."

"Well, help first, then laugh."

Kirk can be a little surly before his first cup of coffee.

"I suppose I could increase the gravity to about 3 G's. That would pull the fan from the ceiling and drop you back on the bed."

"Remember, this fan weighed about twenty pounds at one gravity. It would weigh sixty at three G's. You want that dropping on top of me?"

"Okay, we'll do it the hard way."

I turned off the fan and disentangled my almost-brother along with his blanket.

"Next time, turn off the remote speaker in this room."

"What a novel idea!"

Kirk gradually regained his sunny disposition over breakfast. I even 'cooked' his microwave pancakes and sausage with blueberry topping. I had my usual: two boxes of cold dry

151

cereal with freeze-dried marshmallows washed down by three carafes of coffee directly from the carafe.

"Why do you drink coffee that way?"

"As much as I've lived alone, I've learned to hate washing dishes."

"But with your money now, you could afford a brand-new solid gold coffee mug each time."

"I may have money but I'm.... er, thrifty."

"So, what's the agenda for today?"

"The primary reason for this little jaunt. I want to launch that robot to simulate a supply shuttle. It will hopefully home on a beacon already in place on Earth. If it performs properly, we will be able to keep our starship supplied while traveling."

The robot was about the size of an old-fashioned two-slice toaster but looked a lot like a model of a shuttle from the old Star Trek series minus the engine nacelles.

I'd been saving this as a surprise.

"Kirk, are you ready to go EVA?"

"HUH?" One of his snappy comebacks.

"Extra Vehicular Activity. It means go outside."

'I know what it means but I happen to know we don't have any spacesuits."

"You won't need one. I'll extend a 'shield bubble' from the door. You step outside, place the robot on the ground, and come back inside. I shut down the shield bubble and the robot can go on its merry way."

"What happens if you shut down the bubble too soon?"

"Trust me."

"I remember trusting you several times. I have scars from a few of those times."

"We were kids then. This time, it's life or death."

"Yeah, mine."

"If you do this, I'll let you drive on the way home."

"I'll actually be standing on the surface of the moon with no spacesuit?"

"You sure will. I'll even take pictures."

"Everyone will assume they're fake."

"We'll also shoot a video showing the entire sequence. That would be very difficult to fake."

"Is my life insurance paid up?"

"Do you really care how rich your ex-wives get?"

"Not really, but I care about my kids."

"You know, if anything ever happens to you, here or anyplace else, those kids will never want for anything."

"You mean that?"

"Of course. I know we never spoke it but it's there. We're family."

"Turn on the bubble."

"I'm going to have the bubble 'flicker' just a little so you know exactly where it is. That way, you can avoid going outside it. Just take the robot a couple steps from the *Norton*, place it on the ground, and come right back."

"Can I pose for a picture while I'm out there?"

"Briefly."

He did exactly as instructed. He did, however, manage to hide the robot behind his body while posing so it appeared that he was standing completely alone on the lunar surface.

When Kirk was safely back aboard the ship, I shut down the shield bubble then called Mission Control.

"Operation Shuttle Test is ready to begin."

154

"Acknowledged, *Norton,* beginning countdown."

Mission Control would actually launch the robot remotely. That way, they could have an accurate time record of its travel from lunar surface to the beacon on Earth.

When the countdown reached zero, the robot didn't appear to take off; it simply vanished.

"Where did it go?"

"Earth, I hope…. Star Fleet, are you tracking the robot?"

"We are receiving telemetry but the position data is garbled. Technicians are attempting to decipher it now."

"I suppose all we can do is go about our business."

:"Which is?"

"I want to get high enough above the surface to take a high definition photo of this hemisphere of the moon. It could be valuable for future reference."

We were busily engaged in checking known landmarks to center ourselves over the unmapped part of luna when we received a rather excited call from Mission Control.

"It's HERE!!!!"

"What's there?"

"The robot just landed!"

"It only launched a little over an hour ago."

"Yeah, the professor types tell us it had to have been traveling at more than ten times the speed of light to get here this soon, once you allow for coming halfway around the moon then slowing to mach five through Earth's atmosphere."

"And I didn't even tell it to use full velocity. I believe we have our shuttle system."

The voyage back to Earth was something of an anticlimax. True to my word, I let Kirk drive. It's actually easier than a standard Monty Car because there's not even a beacon to follow until you get close to Earth; just keep Earth centered in the windshield. Once we hit serious atmosphere, I had him slow to mach five and drive it like a Monty Car.

Landing at Star Fleet Headquarters, we were greeted by what seemed to be the same paparazzi and politicians we'd left there when we launched. Of course, in my mind, that type of people are interchangeable.

The press, of course, was clamoring for an interview. I told Roger to plead exhaustion on our part due to the strenuous mission. He was to handle the press. We did have Star Fleet's Press

Corps release selected photos, mostly to prove we had actually been on the moon. The robot test wasn't public knowledge yet.

The next day, I gave orders for work to begin in earnest on Earth's first operational starship along with six supply shuttles. The plans had been completed and the manufacturing facilities were in place but actual construction had been awaiting my order.

That order put thousands of people to work. Not only the ones who were actually constructing the ship and shuttles but the ones fabricating the sub assemblies, making the steel, mining the ore, hauling goods, providing food and other necessary services, and countless other tasks.

Since my discovery put the automobile industry out of business, I had been feeling guilty. I had seriously disrupted the entire world's economy; putting many people out of work. As soon as possible, I had begun creating jobs and I fully intended to continue that practice with the starship business. I discouraged automation in my factories; old-fashioned workmanship turns out better products anyway. There's nothing wrong with power tools, just have a human controlling them.

I didn't shed too many tears over the formerly oil-rich middle-eastern countries that had for many years been breeding grounds for terrorists and constant wars. They were now mostly oil-poor. They could drown in all that

157

nearly worthless oil now; a small amount was used as lubricants and in manufacturing but most countries could produce enough for their own needs.

Terrorism was essentially dead; there were no airliners to bomb and public buildings were universally protected by Montgomery shields. All public figures and many private individuals wore personal armor. How can a terrorist earn a living?

Likewise, war was a moot point. With that option off the board, countries were forced to use words in place of bullets. This was to lead eventually to the effective fall of most national borders and the formation of the World Government. The later introduction of the Arisian Translator sealed the deal. With no borders and no language difficulty, Earth is now becoming one big community.

By the time the *Enterprise* launched, Earth was well on the way to settling down. I hope to continue seeing improvement throughout my lifetime. But I'm not on Earth very much; I spend most of my time aboard my beloved *Enterprise*.

PART TWO

From David A Shaffer:

Regular readers of the Star Tricks series have probably deduced, correctly, that Kirk James is the true author of the books and I merely edit and publish his work.

Kirk sent me the preceding pages but they weren't long enough to compile into book form. You, the reader, wouldn't wish to purchase a book of only about one hundred fifty eight pages. While I was pondering what to do with Kirk's 'mini-missive', I received the following from a surprising source.

I hope you like it as much as I do.

DAS

Exploration Of Ecostria

By

Freedom Marie Johnson James

As many of you will recall, Kirk's last book, Star Tricks: A Funny Thing Happened on The Way to Earth, closed with all of us assembled on Arisia having a good time.

As I begin this narrative, MOST of us continue to have that good time.

I find myself in the tiny minority of one this time.

While I enjoy sex at least as much as anyone else, I find myself becoming jaded and bored with the same acts practiced repeatedly and wish we could get on with some adventure.

I am not at all jealous of Kirk's enjoyment of the other women; I love him dearly and have faith in his love for me. I know that he will be back when he has 'had his fill'.

But I almost wish for some galactic emergency to break up the party.

I find myself spending a lot of time in my communications office, monitoring traffic throughout the galaxy and hoping to pick up the slightest hint of something that would require the presence of Starfleet's Fleet Admiral.

"*Starship Enterprise,* this is Ecostria Planetary Communications."

"Ecostria, this is the *Enterprise.* Go ahead." The on-duty communications officer was doing her job.

"*Enterprise,* this is Rala'K and I would like to speak with Commander Freedom James."

"One moment, please, I will see if she is available."

I keyed the private intercom between my office and the bridge communications station.

"This is Commander James. I'm in my office and heard that. I'll take that call from here."

"Yes, Ma'am."

"Rala'K, this is Freedom James. What can I do for you?"

"Commander James, you may not remember me but I am Admiral K'Ram's mate. We met quite some time ago when the *Enterprise* visited Ecostria."

"Of course I remember you. We had an interesting chat about the unexplored southern half of your planet."

For anyone who has not been reading Kirk's series 'Star Tricks', Ecostria is a planet a very long distance from Earth in the Milky Way near the area we call the Pirate Nebula. Long in the past, Ecostria was nearly split into two halves by some kind of disaster, probably a meteor collision. Now a deep rift divides the northern and southern hemispheres. The northern hemisphere is civilized by a relatively advanced people we have come to know as the Ecostrians.

The Ecostrians strongly resemble the centaurs of Earthly legend; they have a four-legged lower body with a horse-like tail and four hoofed feet. Where a horse's neck would be is a human-like torso with two arms, a neck, and a round head with a face that more-or-less resembles a human face. The Ecostrians were fairly well along in developing technology but not at all interested in space flight or even atmospheric flight until they were invaded by the Feraldi. That story is told in Kirk's books too.

"Exploration of the southern half of the planet is precisely the reason I am calling you. As you know, it's never been done, even though current technology should make it relatively easy. It's always been an interest of mine and a group of others have also agreed to go. The reason I'm calling is to invite you to join us."

"You don't expect to explore half a planet do you?"

"Certainly not! We just wish to travel to an interesting area in the interior and look around."

"Will K'Ram be going?"

"No, he won't. In fact, this will be an all-female expedition. The males have long acted as if we females are incapable of anything but child care and housework. This is our chance to demonstrate our worth."

"On my world, the struggle for female equality was long and difficult. Even now, with powerful laws enforcing equal rights, some males still consider females to be inferior. I'll be happy to help you. When do you plan to begin?"

"We have most of the equipment assembled and the people are beginning to arrange to have time from their various duties but it appears we won't be able to begin for about ten standard days."

"Great! That will give me time to make my arrangements and then to get there. I'll see you in a few days."

At that time, I was on Arisia and Ecostria was approximately sixty light years distant. I had no idea HOW I was going but I was going.

"Take the *Anne McCaffrey*." Kirk wasn't being difficult about this at all; I had expected some resistance.

"By myself?"

"Why not? Star Fleet will supply a complete remote crew so you won't even need to pilot if you don't want to. Just relax and enjoy the ride."

"And you won't mind me being gone for a while?"

"Not at all. Of course I'll miss you but I've been partying pretty hard lately and I can see that you're not enjoying yourself. Go have some fun."

That's Kirk for you. Just as I was working up to get mad at him, he totally disarmed me. And I doubt he even knew that he did it. He was just being his own sweet self.

Because sexual 'treats' would be gilding the lily, I gave him a nice kiss and began planning for my adventure.

Number one on any woman's list is what to wear. In this case, it would be sturdy, comfortable clothing that could possibly protect me from harsh environments. I expected to be using a personal Montgomery shield but you never know.

Add in two spare sets of prosthetic legs. They're easy to pack; looking much like old-fashioned panty girdles with small bulges for the electronics.

After a little thought, I decided to take a force blade. I usually dislike carrying weapons but the force blade is small and easy to carry. For those of you who haven't read Kirk's books, a force blade is a handle about one and a half inches in diameter and eighteen inches long. When activated, it projects a force field about a meter long and only about a molecule thick but very stiff. This field is surrounded by a blue glow that serves as a warning to help prevent accidents. The force blades are strongly reminiscent of light sabers from Star Wars.

"Maybe you should take this too." I was talking to Damien Daniel, the head of the computer maintenance department of the *Enterprise*. Damien is a good friend and swinging partner. His Apache heritage is prominent in his high cheekbones and the traditional 'pigtails' he wears.

He offered me a sheathed knife.

"What's this?"

"It's called a K-Bar. I ordered it online for my knife collection but the handle is too small for my hand. It should be just right for you."

"But I don't know anything about knife fighting."

"It's a very handy all-around tool and last-resort weapon. But just in case you do need it as a weapon, I'll give you a crash course."

Well, OK."

"The first thing to remember is that a knife isn't a stabbing weapon; it's a cutting weapon. Cut your opponent and try for something vital. On a human, it's a soft target like the throat. But keep cutting. On an unknown alien, you can only guess but try to find something vulnerable. If nothing else, remove its ability to harm you."

"I'm not sure I can be that vicious."

"If you're down to fighting with the K-Bar, its kill or be killed. Don't pull any punches."

After that, he taught me how to sharpen the K-Bar using the whetstone that rode in it's own part of the knife sheath.

"Remember, a dull knife is a dangerous knife. Keep it razor-sharp."

Damien is one of our favorite swinging partners and he had just been very helpful; I spent the next couple of hours 'thanking' him.

The supply department had a backpack that just comfortably held all the things I was planning to take. Kirk is always teasing me about the 'girl stuff' I habitually carry in my purse but most of that would be left behind; I

169

didn't expect to encounter any humans or anyone else to impress so my makeup and other preening accessories would be left behind. I would only take a small hair pick for my short 'fro.

The supply officer even graciously included a tiny field-powered gravity device that made the pack weigh exactly zero at one standard Earth gravity and could be adjusted to lift me above obstacles if I wished. Because my personal Montgomery shield could also 'fly' me, I thought this would be unnecessary but it was a nice touch. The tiny control panel was affixed to the strap of the backpack.

I didn't expect to use many of these 'super gadgets' because the Ecostrians wouldn't have such things and it wouldn't be fair to 'wimp out' in front of them. However, they all have four very strong legs and are accustomed to using them for long periods. My two prosthetic legs don't get tired but the remainder of my body does.

In a message to Ecostria, I had asked about food. Rala'K had replied that we would be carrying sufficient food, suitable for both Ecostrian and human, to last for at least twenty days. In addition, two members of the party were experts on edible plants and wildlife.

So I couldn't think of any other bases to cover. I had transportation, clothing, and food taken care of. Kirk was content here on Arisia and it appeared he would be busy for quite some time. The galaxy in general was quiet as could be.

"Hon, I'm leaving for Ecostria tomorrow."

"Okay, great. I hope you have fun."

"I'll only be a communicator call away if you need me."

"The same for me. If you run into anything you can't handle, just call and the whole fleet will be on the way, if needed."

Our lovemaking that night was sweet but seemed to lack the usual fire. I think all his recent activity was taking the 'edge' off him. I hoped it was only temporary.

****

"Ecostria Approach Control, this is Battle Tank *Anne McCaffrey*."

"*Anne McCaffrey,* this is Ecostria, go ahead."

"We show an ETA of about one hour."

"Acknowledged, *McCaffrey*, the beacon you are following will take you directly to your intended destination. Our planetary shield will be opened for your arrival."

The expedition would be assembling in the city where we first met M'Bing, one of the leaders of the resistance that opposed the Feraldi

171

invasion. M'Bing now lived on Earth, working for Kirk's brother on a horse and pony ranch in Wyoming.

Because the Ecostrians had never used aircraft; going directly from no flight to using captured Feraldi field vehicles, they had no airports. The beacon led us directly to the building where the expedition was assembling.

I thanked the remote crew of the *Anne McCaffrey*; they were composed of senior Star Fleet Academy students and had performed perfectly. The trusty battle tank would now be shut down until I needed it for my return home.

Rala'K herself was waiting to greet me when I exited the ship. I have trouble distinguishing one Ecostrian from another but I remembered her distinctive white tail.

She. However, seemed to remember me quite well.

"Free, I'm so happy you chose to join our little expedition."

"It's high time we females show the males we're more than decorations."

"Precisely! We had some difficulty obtaining permission for this trip but the Planetary Council in the end could find no valid excuse to deny us. We're well supplied and supported and with you along, we even have interplanetary support."

172

"How many persons will be going?"

"We decided to keep the group fairly small. Other than you and me, there will be five others. As I mentioned, two are experts at edible plants and wildlife. One is an experienced builder and two are medical people. All are in excellent physical condition."

"Is much known of the area where we are going?"

"Only from aerial photographs. We picked an area that looks interesting in a mountainous region. The area has mostly forest with ample water but no true jungle. Photos taken from the air have shown large unidentified animals but we have no idea if they might be dangerous. Even many of the trees are unfamiliar to us."

"So this will be a lot like visiting an unknown planet."

"Exactly. However, we can be almost certain of finding edible wildlife and plants. Also, if we run into trouble, we can call for help and be rescued in a very short time. Rescue shuttles are to be staffed and ready at all times. Each of us will carry a 'panic button' box. If you activate the box, a shuttle will be dispatched to pick you up and carry you to safety very quickly."

"One thing I'm curious about is your name. Did it just happen to be similar to K'Ram's?"

"No, my name was originally S'Meara but when I mated with K'Ram, I changed it to resemble his. It's the custom on this world."

"I see. My name was originally Freedom Johnson but according to our custom I changed it to Freedom James when we mated."

"So the customs aren't terribly different."

"When an Ecostrian, M'Bing, married an Earth pony with only one simple name, Daisy, she began calling herself Daisy M'Bing. I rather like that."

"I know M'Bing and met Daisy when they were here to be married. She is a delightful person."

"I agree. Perhaps you should introduce me to the rest of the expedition party."

"Of course. They are all inside and waiting to meet you."

She led me inside to where five other Ecostrians waited. Unlike Earth people, Ecostrians don't rest on furniture; when relaxing, they just 'splay' all four legs, lock the knees, and rest.

Rala'K introduced me to Mal'D and Reg'N, the medical people, Gen'E and Ming'R were their world's equivalent of survivalists, experts at 'living off the land'. The group was completed by Han'A, who had worked alongside her mate for many years in the building trade.

I tried to find distinctive features to help me remember the names of my new friends and companions. I've always had trouble distinguishing one Ecostrian from another by facial features and they don't wear clothing. All are covered by horse-like hair from the withers down but in a uniformly chestnut brown. I just hoped I'd learn in time.

For the edification of you 'horndogs' out there (myself included), I asked Rala'K about the breasts that all the females proudly displayed. Yes, Ecostrians suckle their young and yes, the females enjoy having the breasts fondled. But no thought is ever given to hiding or covering the breasts except to protect them from cold or injury.

The Ecostrians would be carrying their 'packs' as saddlebags in clever harnesses that draped just behind the human-like upright torsos. These could easily be reached by twisting the torso without removing the pack.

The plan was for us to be taken in four shuttle vehicles to a pre-selected location on the southern hemisphere. There, the all-female crews of the shuttles would set up and maintain a base camp while we, the true expedition, continued on foot to do the actual exploring. The shuttle crews were to monitor our 'panic button' frequencies at all times and be ready to come to our aid at any time. Other rescue personnel would also be standing by on the northern hemisphere but necessarily further away.

"Very well. The time here is late afternoon but the area where we are going is in a different time zone so it won't be dawn there for about seven hours. I suggest that everyone rest or sleep as much as possible. We'll leave in about five hours and that will have us arriving at our base camp area in the early morning."

She got me aside. "Free, I know you need to lie down to sleep and there is a good place for that in a room over here. It has a soft couch and it should be dark and fairly quiet."

"Thank you for your thoughtfulness. I'm not sure I can sleep with all the excitement and after all the sleeping I did on the trip here but I'll try."

Surprisingly, I slept rather quickly. It seemed like only a couple minutes later when Rala'K was gently shaking my shoulder.

"Free, it's about time to board the shuttles."

"Oh, okay, let me use the facilities and I'll be right there."

Ecostrians use a completely different type of indoor plumbing but I've learned to adapt on earlier visits to that planet. Fortunately, they use similar washing arrangements so I was able to splash my face with cold water as well as wash my hands.

Ecostrian shuttles are much larger than those manufactured on Earth. I suppose they need more room to move around because they can't sit and standing in a single position would be very tiring. They had, however, provided a nicely padded chair for me so I rode in comfort. The pilot and navigator were provided with clever padded braces that allowed them to rest or stand at will while operating their controls.

The area chosen for our base camp was a sizable clearing in what could have been an impressive first-growth forest on Earth. The trees were unfamiliar to me but only of a moderate density with light undergrowth near the clearing. It could easily have been a pleasant forest scene on Earth except for the lack of birds and flying insects.

The shuttles landed in a circular formation to form the base camp. We, the expedition, filed off with our equipment while the shuttle crews began setting up a semi-permanent camp.

"Okay, Ladies, we should be well-rested and ready to begin exploring. We have no accurate maps of this area but you have each been issued a compass and direction finder that will direct you back to this clearing in case you become separated from the group. We all have communicators to remain in contact with each other or with base camp or even the outside world if necessary. The plan calls for us to begin walking in a southerly direction. That will bring us, eventually, to a moderately-sized mountain range. We will undoubtedly be unable to scale any mountains but we'll see plenty along the way. Take plenty of pictures and if you see anything really interesting, be sure to tell all of us. There's no need to hurry so take your time and anyone can ask for a break at any time."

"What about hostile wildlife?" I didn't have the names straight so I wasn't sure who asked this but I thought it was a good question.

"We have no idea what animals we might encounter here. You each have a Star Fleet-issue phaser that should be capable of stopping any animal we encounter. Just point it and push both buttons. Most of us dislike violence against any living beings so we didn't bring lethal weapons." I thought it best not to mention my force blade and if anyone noticed, it could be passed off as a tool.

"Are there any other questions?" She paused, giving us all time to think. "Okay, let's move out."

Rala'K began leading us into the forest at an easy pace in a southerly direction.

Once we were well into the trees, it was much darker than I had thought while standing in the clearing but after some time, my eyes adjusted and I could see fairly well. Visibility was limited due to the trees anyway; we couldn't see very far into the distance and had to rely on the compass for direction.

The terrain was relatively level with only a few boulders we must step around so we were able to maintain a fairly straight course.

Once again, I was surprised at the lack of flowering plants but reminded myself that this world had no flying creatures of any kind; pollination was accomplished by crawling insects and wind-blown pollen so flowers had never developed. Many plants had large, sticky, 'receptacles' for receiving pollen but they weren't colorful or decorative.

Gen'E and Ming'R were foraging for edible bits to add to our ration packs as we walked. Rala'K had asked them to do this as the rations were sufficient to keep us alive but not really all we might want. The survival experts were certain they could supplement the basic diet admirably.

My communicator beeped.

"Everyone, this is Rala'K, we need someone with a large, very sharp knife here at the front of our advance. Ming'R has found a treat for us."

Thinking of the K-Bar that Damien had given me, I hurried forward.

It didn't take long to find the others assembling around Ming'R, who had discovered a small stream or creek. Her attention was focused on something in the water.

"I have a very good knife here." I displayed the K-Bar.

"Very good. Attached to the rocks, just below water level, are three behortas. They need to be harvested by cutting about the width of your finger from the rock. No closer to the rock, please."

"You want me to do it?"

"If you would, please. It's very difficult for any of us to bend that low and it's your knife anyway."

"Exactly what are these behortas and why do we want to cut them?"

"They are a lower form of animal life. They form a very hard shell and fill it with almost pure protein. All of their vital organs are located in the 'foot' which is near the rock. If you cut as I described, the carcass will need very little further preparation before cooking and eating."

"Can't we just pull them free then cut them up here?"

"They make a very powerful waterproof glue. Once it leaves the 'foot', it reacts with water and forms an almost unbreakable bond with rock or any other surface. I doubt that all of us together could pull one free."

Not fully convinced, I peered into the water. Just below the waterline were three humps that I thought were rocks at first but on closer inspection decided they were too regular.

Inspecting them more closely, they looked more like World War Two army helmets.

"You're sure they don't bite or anything?"

"They have no defensive systems; they rely on their shells."

So I tentatively reached into the water and slipped the blade of the K-Bar between the shell of the nearest behorta and its supporting rock.

Using a slight sawing motion I quickly separated the behorta from the rock.

Ming'R inspected it.

"Not bad at all. You got a little of its organs with it but it's a matter of experience. If you look here, this is one of its glue-producing organs. Be careful; if any gets on you, it will just need to wear away in time; no known solvent will remove it. We'll finish trimming this one after you harvest the others."

So I went back and got the others, being careful to cut a little further from the rock. Ming'R was satisfied.

"These will keep unrefrigerated for at least a day but I'm sure we'll eat them tonight. Once we make sure all the organs are trimmed, we only need to roast the shells. The meat inside cooks free of the shell and is very tasty and nutritious."

We continued along, observing our surroundings and watching as the survival experts found more things for our dinner, occasionally sharing a tidbit with some of us and teaching us about edible plants.

"What about meat?" Someone asked.

Gen'E answered that one. "There are many species of edible wildlife. Unfortunately, I haven't seen many of them and the ones I have seen would be difficult to obtain. I've seen evidence of cabrana in the area and while they are edible, they are difficult to kill, hard to prepare, and frankly, taste terrible. I've seen glimpses of animals I didn't recognize a couple times but I have no idea if they are suitable as food sources."

"Also, we have no hunting equipment." I pointed out.

"That would be no problem if we cared to set up snares or other proper traps." Ming'R told me. "But that would require us to remain in

182

one area for quite some time. Perhaps when we stop for the night."

As we walked, the terrain was becoming more rugged and the trees were becoming thinner. The underbrush was much less dense and it was my guess that we were approaching the foothills to the mountainous region.

Late in the afternoon we made a discovery that chilled me to the bone. We came upon the carcass of a large animal, easily the size of an Earthly elephant and roughly the same shape but lacking a trunk and possessing six legs. The beast was obviously a meat-eater, judging from the shape of its jaw and teeth but what distressed all of us were the wounds that apparently had killed it.

This beast had very obviously been killed and partially consumed by a large, clawed predator.

"What is that and what killed it?"

"I've never seen an animal like that and the marks on it are foreign to me." Rala'K had to admit.

The wildlife experts were quick to agree.

Noting something odd about the creature's skin, I tried the K-Bar on it. I had great difficulty penetrating the skin with the K-Bar even when using all the force of my body

183

weight. Now, that K-Bar has a VERY sharp point and blade. With my body weight behind it, I should have been able to penetrate even an elephant's skin with little difficulty.

I finally drew my force blade and cut a large sample free of the carcass for later study. The meat inside the skin had long been carted away by scavengers, leaving only the skin and bones. The skin was paper-thin but very tough and resilient.

The skin was so tough that it retained its shape and refused to roll into a small package to fit my pack. I was forced to cut it into several small pieces with the force blade.

"Perhaps we should move along but everyone make sure you know where your phasers are." Rala'K now seemed apprehensive.

For anyone who hasn't read my husband's Star Tricks series, a phaser is a small gizmo that looks a lot like an old remote garage door opener. If you point it at a person (or animal) and push two buttons, it will enclose your target in a force field. You can then hold the target as long as necessary or use the anti-gravity feature to move it anywhere you wish before releasing it.

Now, the group moved through the forest in a stealthier manner, looking around more carefully and several people were holding phasers in their hands. I decided to activate my personal force field even though none of the

184

others had that luxury. "What the heck, they can't tell I'm using it." I thought.

Eventually, it was beginning to become dark and we reached a nicely-sized clearing with a small stream flowing past.

"This looks like a lovely place to camp for the night." Rala'K declared.

No one seemed inclined to argue, least of all myself. While my legs are prosthetic and powered, they are attached to muscle-and-bone thighs and hips; I was getting tired.

As the 'outdoorsy' types prepared dinner, the medical people came around making sure no one needed medical attention. I didn't have any complaints so they moved on after a short chat.

Gen'E and Ming'R had prepared a stew by roasting the behortas in the fire until the meat came free of the shells. They then cut the meat into bite-sized pieces and added it to the many different vegetables they had collected along the way and concocted a delicious stew. An assortment of wild herbs added a great spicy flavor. This was so good that nobody even suggested opening a prepared ration pack.

The behorta meat had an unusual flavor. It wasn't fishy and no, it didn't taste like chicken. It had a subtle taste of its own that I just can't describe but I liked it and I'll be happy to eat it again any time.

185

By the time we finished eating and washing up, full dark had fallen.

"We might as well get some sleep. I'll activate a force field to cover the entire clearing so we won't need to stand guard duty. I want everyone to be well-rested in the morning. I'll wake everyone at first light and we'll eat before moving on."

As I've mentioned before, Ecostrians sleep standing but I needed to lie down to sleep. I had brought a powered sleeping bag for this purpose. This little gem had a Montgomery field-powered compressor that kept a thin air mattress inflated to keep my body insulated from the ground. That same field provided gravity-reduction to make sleeping more comfortable and would also shield me from the elements and wildlife if that were necessary. Being quite thin when deactivated, it took up very little room in my pack. I moved to the edge of the clearing to avoid being accidentally stepped on in the dark.

I woke in pitch dark, lying on the hard, chilly ground. An unknown insect was crawling on my face and I could hear the voices of the others raised in a confused panic.

"Something is not right." I told myself. (A shrewd deduction)

I struggled into my prosthetic leg support system but when I activated it, nothing happened. Reaching into my pack for a Montgomery-powered flashlight, I discovered that it wouldn't work either. Checking my Montgomery-powered wristwatch confirmed my growing suspicion: all Montgomery fields had failed us. This meant that we had no power for most of our communications or defensive devices. Even our navigation equipment, other than simple compasses, would be useless.

And I couldn't walk.

Even if I had one of my wheelchairs, it would be helpless in this environment. And the nearest manual wheelchair was some sixty lightyears away on Arisia.

"Rala'K, I need some help!"

She came over, carrying a makeshift torch from the campfire.

"What's wrong?"

"My prosthetic legs won't work. I've tried and all the devices powered by energy-gathering fields are inoperable. Unless they begin working again, I'm going to have a problem."

"We noticed the problem with the powered devices but I hadn't thought about your legs. We'll need to find some way to help you move. Remember, the protective screen failed too and whatever predator killed that large animal could be out there."

Great, I hadn't thought about that complication.

187

"Do we have any kind of weapons at all?"

"No, a couple of the ladies are completely against violence; even for hunting and self-defense. We decided to rely on the phasers and force fields but neither is working now."

"So at present, we can't run and we can't fight."

"That is a very astute summary of the situation."

"How about hiding?"

"We can probably find someplace to hide for a while but any predator out there is at home in this environment; we're the visitors here and we have only a limited amount of food while he or it has the entire forest."

"How long until someone comes looking for us?"

"We were expected to call with a progress report tomorrow. If we miss a day or two, someone will probably start to look, but will rescue vehicles work? And even if they do, how will they find us in this forest without communicators?"

"So our best bet is to find some way to defend ourselves then retrace our path to base camp."

"That is what I had in mind. I'll put it to the others but I doubt that anyone else will have a better idea."

"I can 'walk' a little on my leg stumps but not far."

"I've seen pictures from your planet of humans riding animals called horses. Have you ever done that?"

"Yes I have, a few times."

"Do you think you could ride on my back?"

"I'm sure I could but my weight would tire you quickly."

"I hope that the others will offer to take turns but I can see no other way of moving this group."

So I quickly packed my gear, abandoning everything I was sure we could do without in order to save weight.

When I was packed, Rala'K knelt as much as possible and gave me a 'hand up' while I stood on my leg stumps and pulled myself up on her back, mostly by sheer arm strength.

She struggled back to her feet.

"A true riding horse on Earth is larger and stronger than you. And we use padded devices called saddles to make it more comfortable for both horse and rider."

"Well, we must do what we can. I'm sure I can carry you for quite some distance if I don't have to run."

"Without legs to grip your body, I'm not sure I could stay up here if you ran."

"Feel free to hold my shoulders if you need to."

With her upright human-like torso in front of me, it was rather like riding as passenger on a motorcycle. But I had no legs or feet to brace myself so I had to steady myself with my hands.

Walking over to the others, Rala'K made sure they had their gear packed.

"Now, we need to move from this area. After the evidence we saw of a large predator and due to our lack of defenses or weapons, I think we should try to retrace our steps to the base camp. Also, as distasteful as some may find it, we should think about devising some kind of weapons to defend ourselves from predators."

No one took issue with that.

Ming'R spoke: "I noticed some ewealla bushes not long before we stopped for the night. The single upright main stem usually makes an excellent bow but they are often too strong for most people to pull."

"And I saw a large stand of cawalla weeds. The stems grow very long, straight, and tough. I'm sure they would make excellent arrows."

"I don't approve of violence or weapons." Added Gen'E. "But I believe the sinews from that large animal carcass we saw yesterday would make excellent bowstrings."

"Now, we'll need arrowheads, nocks, and a way of fastening everything together."

"Nocks?" Rala'K was puzzled.

"The nock is the notched piece at the tail of the arrow where the bowstring engages it. You can carve it into the wood of the arrow but that will often split. A better method is to carve it from bone or other strong material." Gen'E explained.

"Well, that large creature had plenty of bone. But can anyone do such carving?" Rala'K asked.

It turned out that Mal'D's hobby was carving intricate miniatures. She had brought a small set of carving tools in case she got the chance to whittle something. Now she certainly would. "Just show me what we need."

"Now we need arrowheads and some kind of vanes."

I actually got a chance to contribute. "I believe that the skin of that large animal would

191

make excellent vanes; it's very rigid and resumes its shape after being bent; it's thin and tough."

"But how will we get all these pieces to stay together?"

"Behorta cement." I stated simply. "And I believe we can carve arrowheads from behorta shells."

"And have the meat as a bonus! Excellent idea, Free. If no one else has anything to add, I suggest we start moving."

So we set out, moving in a northerly direction and trying to retrace our earlier path.

But this time, we were trying to be much more observant. Any sudden sound in the forest would cause us all to freeze and hold our breaths.

Not far along our path, we found the euealla bushes. The survivalists borrowed my K-Bar to harvest and trim several likely-looking stems. I was a little dubious as those potential 'bows' looked terribly strong.

Not much further along, we found the cawalla weeds. These looked a lot like cat-tail plants from Earth but after the survivalists harvested a big bundle I examined one and found the stem to be very strong and tough, almost like wood.

"Shouldn't we have daylight by now?" Gen'E voiced my question well.

The sky was nearly as dark now as it had been when I discovered that our powered devices weren't working, even though that had been several hours ago.

Most of the others had timepieces utilizing powered fields but Reg'N had an antique: a watch powered by batteries.

Ecostrians use a different system for keeping time but Reg'N's watch confirmed that the sun should have risen several hours earlier. Indeed, if we looked carefully, we could see a slightly lighter spot in the sky at the location we all felt the sun should be.

"I've never seen overcast like this." Rala'K commented.

The others agreed.

"Do you think we'll need to deal with a storm along with all our other problems?" I worried.

"It doesn't feel like stormy weather; the humidity and the general 'feel' of things just don't add up to a storm. However, there is a strange smell in the air that wasn't there yesterday. I don't know if it's connected to our problem or not."

By now, we had covered a considerable distance even though the darkness

193

was necessarily hindering our progress. Our lack of sightseeing probably made up for that.

It did seem that all of us could see slightly better. I'm not sure if our eyes were adapting or the light was subtly improving but all of us could see objects quite some distance away, if dimly.

Due to this, the group had spread out a little. Rala'K, as usual, was in the lead with me on her back. The survival experts were flanking us slightly to the rear and sides with the medical personnel behind them and Han'A, the builder, was bringing up the rear.

"Aaaaaaaaaaaaaaaaaaaa!!!!!...HELP!!!!!" From the rear.

We turned and rushed to Han'A to find her engaged in a one-sided battle with a nightmare creature.

The creature looked a little like a mountain lion but had very shaggy fur and, being a native of Ecostria, it had six legs. It fought standing on four legs while using the two forelegs as weapons. It had pounced on Han'A when she unwittingly wandered under a large tree. She was now streaming blood from several deep gashes in her back.

Han'A had been carrying the bundle of potential bows and was now using one as a club. It was doing little damage but the cat-thing was attempting to avoid blows from the club while stalking her.

The others, having no better weapons, picked up large rocks and began pelting the cat-thing. They were doing little damage but the beast didn't like it.

I couldn't bend far enough to pick up rocks so the only thing I could do was think.

Then it came to me: my force blade was powered by a small battery and only recharged by a Montgomery field. It should operate; at least for a short while.

I reached into my pack and pulled out the handle. Operating the switch briefly confirmed my memory; the blade would function.

"Rala'K, carry me quickly past that thing. Make sure to pass so it's on our left side." I'm left-handed.

To Rala'K's credit, she didn't ask questions. She did a fair imitation of a medieval knight's charger and carried me past the beast at a full gallop.

Holding Rala'K's shoulder with my right hand, I swung the force blade with my left hand.

My aim wasn't perfect but I managed to carve a large chunk from the beast's skull. When Rala'K came to a halt and turned for another pass, the creature was lying on the ground, twitching.

I turned off the force blade to save the battery.

Mal'D and Reg'N, being medical people, began treating Han'A's wounds. The rest of us, having nothing better to do, had moderate to severe hysterics.

Rala'K recovered first.

"All right, Ladies, That's enough. There could be more of those things out there and we need to be ready for the next one. How is Han'A?"

"The wounds are deep but no important muscles were damaged. She'll be sore for several days but she should be able to walk."

"Thank you, Mal'D. And Free, I'm certainly glad you were with us. I doubt any of us could have stopped that thing."

"My force blade is only operating on limited battery power; we need to build other weapons very soon."

"Very well. As soon as possible, we'll move on to the site of that carcass where we can obtain the remainder of our weapon material."

"Remember, we need some behortas too."

"They seem plentiful in the streams here. We can use the meat as well."

"By the way, what was that beast?"

"It looked a little like a maraowi but it was much larger than any I've ever seen. And whatever was responsible for that carcass we found must have been even larger."

"Perhaps we should be moving instead of talking."

"Excellent idea."

We pushed on, gathering behortas along the way and finding the huge carcass with little difficulty.

Mal'D had obtained a good supply of bone at the carcass and was producing arrow knocks. Ming'R began carving arrowheads from the behorta shells. Han'A, despite her wounds, was able to make bows from the ewealla stems. I was putting the arrows together using behorta glue.

But when finished, the bows were far too stiff for any of us to pull.

"These bows should be very powerful if we could only use them."

"And the arrows are very long and straight with sharp, deadly heads. They'll make excellent weapons, both for defense and hunting.

197

Now we only need to find a way to use the bows."

I remembered when the *Enterprise* had visited the planet Goya. That planet is governed by women and even the warriors there are women. Their primary weapon is a crossbow.

"Can you build some of these?" I sketched out what I had in mind, using my note pad.

Keeping the design simple, it didn't take long. We built crossbows with a long lever for cocking the string. I estimated that they had a 'pull' of about two hundred pounds and a string travel of about eighteen inches. The arrows or 'bolts' were nearly a meter long and tipped with razor-sharp triangular heads; rather like a deer arrow.

While the arrowheads were being whittled, we were all practicing with sharpened sticks for bolts. Everyone was able to cock and fire a crossbow but accuracy was an individual skill.

While the crafty people were making the crossbows and bolts, I used some of the 'elephant hide' and some thin, stout cord to construct slings, much as the biblical David used. With practice, any of us could hurl a fist-sized rock at a considerable velocity. Again, accuracy was an individual thing and a matter of dedication. Surprisingly, Gen'E became very good with hers in spite of being abysmal with a crossbow.

We had camped for two days near the carcass but all felt the time was well-spent. By the time we were ready to move on, each of us was armed with a sling, a crossbow, and ten bolts. Each also carried a few nicely-sized rocks for the slings but we were sure we could find more as needed.

We had only been traveling a couple of hours when we came upon a large meadow. The tree line was visible in the distance so we knew this wasn't the end of the forest but it was a welcome change.

"Well, Ladies, should we walk across or stay in the trees and walk around?" I believe that Rala'K was concerned about meeting a predator in the meadow.

"Let's walk across. It will save time and there's less chance of entering the forest at the wrong place." I think Han'A's wounds were making her impatient.

No one else commented so we set out across the meadow.

We hadn't walked far when a grey-brown streak broke from the forest behind us and some distance to our left.

Whatever it was traveled too quickly to be seen clearly but almost directly in front of us and about fifty feet away, it stopped.

"What is that?"

"I've never seen anything like it, Free. Has anyone else?" Rala'K was as surprised as I.

The others all expressed negative replies.

The creature we were viewing was about the size of a large dog with grey-brown shaggy hair and a bushy tail. It had the usual six legs for this planet but the four front legs were straight, much like the two front legs of an Earthly dog or cat. When the creature walked casually, it used these four legs. But the hindmost two legs were like a jackrabbit: very large and built for jumping. When the creature was walking slowly, these legs and feet failed to touch the ground. We had no doubt that these jumping legs were resting now and would be used when the creature chose to move quickly.

The creature began eating heartily from the underbrush.

"Why isn't it afraid of us?"

"It probably thinks we're a small herd of fellow plant-eaters." Rala'K had the very likely answer.

"Do you suppose it's good to eat?"

"Most plant-eaters are." Supplied Ming'R. "If it doesn't eat us, we can eat it."

"Behorta meat is good but I'm beginning to tire of it."

"We might as well try something different."

Ming'R had proven to be the best shot with the crossbow so she was chosen to take the first shot at the creature.

The bolt skewered the creature through the neck, badly wounding it but it was still able to move. Strangely, it didn't run away but staggered around, apparently confused. A fist-sized rock from Gen'E's sling finished the job.

As Ming'R was field-dressing our prize, we were discussing what to call this unknown creature.

"I think it should be called a veloci-hopper." I stated.

They looked at me in puzzlement.

"In my native language, the prefix, 'veloci' means 'fast' and of course, 'hopper' is obvious."

They all 'tried the name on for size' and liked it.

"I think this will make an excellent stew along with some of the vegetables and herbs we can pick up along the trail." Ming'R had the meat ready to go.

"We'll stop in a while to eat some of the packaged rations. In the mean time, don't be shy about snacking on the things our experts have shown us in the forest."

I will say that I was never especially hungry on this trip; the experts showed us many edible vegetables and fruits and the evening meals were excellent. When necessary, the packaged rations weren't too bad, either.

"Unless we're badly off course, we should reach base camp tomorrow."

"If they're still there."

"If their equipment has also failed, they won't be able to leave, either. But they should have more supplies and any rescue will know where to look."

When it was just past mid-day by Reg'N's watch, Rala'K called a halt and we broke out the ration packs. Most of us had been snacking along the way on nuts and berries we found so very few rations were consumed but the rest was welcomed. Of course, I had been riding on Rala'K's back but the chance to get down and move around a little was welcome also.

After our lunch break we moved on, still keeping to our southerly course and trying to remember our former path as well as possible.

"To be honest, I wasn't paying much attention to our route that first day because I was counting on our electronic equipment to show us the way back." Rala'K admitted.

Even the survival experts confessed to the same 'crime'; they hadn't given much thought to our course.

So now we were attempting to find base camp by dead reckoning. I personally believe it's called dead reckoning because if you reckon wrong, you're dead.

But there was no doubt that we were much closer to base camp than we were two days ago so I suppose that can be called progress.

It may have been my imagination but I believe that the sky was a little less dark that afternoon. When I asked Rala'K, she wasn't sure but thought I could be right. Looking around, we were able to see our entire group and a considerable amount of the surrounding forest. But the trees prevented sight for any real distance no matter the light conditions so it was difficult to say.

"AAAAAAAAAAAAAAAA!"

"AAAAAAAAAAAAAAA!"

The screams didn't harmonize well but I wasn't going to reprimand Ming'R and Gen'E. We hurried to find the source of their dismay.

When Rala'K and I arrived near them, we saw the most bizarre creature we had yet encountered.

This one had four 'walking legs' as well as two 'grasping legs' that had specialized into vicious claws, much like an Earthly lobster. The creature also had a long segmented tail curled above its back much like the scorpion of Earth. It had a large, roundish head with eyes on short stalks and large horizontal mandibles. The entire beast was about six feet long and maybe two feet high at the back. It was covered in what appeared to be armor or chitin.

"Does anyone know what it is?" Rala'K asked.

"Earth has something like it called a scorpion but ours are much smaller." Was the best I could do.

"How dangerous is the one on your planet?"

"The sting in it's tail is poisonous but rarely deadly. The ones on Earth aren't large enough to be a threat with their claws. But this one looks big enough to sting, bite, or claw any of us to death."

Mal'D, ever the scientist, asked me, "What kind of venom does Earth's scorpion have?"

"I believe I read someplace that it's a mixture of enzyme inhibitors and neurotoxins but this creature probably isn't even remotely related."

"Quite right. And that sting looks capable of injecting a very large quantity of whatever venom it produces. I'm sure we want no part of any of it."

During this discussion, the others were regaining at least a little composure.

"Should we kill it?" Ming'R wanted to know.

"I hate to let anything that ugly live. And it could be a threat behind us. See if you can kill it with your crossbow." Rala'K made the decision.

But crossbow bolts only deflected from the thing's armor. And if it had seemed short-tempered before, now it was positively enraged.

"Does anyone have an idea?"

"I guess I'll have to use my force blade." I was reluctant, both to face the creature that closely and to use precious battery power.

"How do you want to do this?"

"Some of you get its attention; taunt it but stay out of it's reach. While it's paying attention to you, Rala'K can sneak me around behind it and I'll chop off its stinger. After that, we'll deal with its claws."

So that's what we did. Gen'E nearly got too close and the 'scorpion' almost got her with its stinger but as it was cocking for another strike, I lopped off its tail.

This set the thing into a frenzy. We all withdrew until it settled down some then Rala'K carried me near enough to lop off first one claw then the other. The creature didn't move much after that so I chopped off its head to be certain.

Its legs were still twitching feebly but none of us could see how the creature could present a further danger to us.

"Does anyone want to try eating that?" I hope Ming'R was joking.

"I suppose it would be something like the shrimp from my world." I was trying to get into the spirit of the jest.

"I've heard of Earth's shrimp. I suspect that this animal is warm-blooded. I note that it has red blood and the supporting organs appear to be less insect-like than I first imagined." Mal'D observed.

"Perhaps we should simply leave this one where it is. I'm anxious to get moving anyway." Rala'K settled that one.

We didn't get much further that day. Between the excitement and the exertion, everyone was soon ready to settle down for the night.

And I've failed to mention that the day sky was now decidedly lighter than the night sky. We still couldn't see far but visibility was improving. Either whatever was blocking the sun was lightening or we were adapting.

"Rala'K, are you going to keep Free to yourself for this entire trip?"

"That wasn't my intent; I merely hesitated to cause a burden for anyone else."

"If she agrees, I'd like to carry her tomorrow."

"You will get no argument from me, Ming'R. What do you say, Free?"

Ming'R was actually larger than Rala'K but I had hesitated to suggest any changes.

"I only wish I were capable of walking for myself but I will happily allow Ming'R to carry me with many thanks to Rala'K."

So when we resumed our trek in the morning, I was astride Ming'R.

"Do you find this as pleasant as I?"

"What do you mean?" We had been traveling for several hours now and Ming'R and I had been getting to know each other by chatting.

"I know that your genitals are rubbing against my back. I can't feel that but thinking about it is very stimulating."

"At times, the motion becomes stimulating for me, too but I try not to think about it because there's nothing to be done about it."

"I've heard that some Human females enjoy pleasing each other."

"I do that quite frequently."

"How do you do that?" She was almost panting now.

I shrugged. "We kiss, we fondle each other's breasts, we touch each other all over; we use our mouths."

"Do you ever use artificial aids?"

"At times."

She was staggering and stumbling slightly now. I sincerely hoped no emergencies presented themselves.

"Would you consider playing with me?"

208

I looked at her. Ecostrians aren't Human. They have two eyes, one nose, one mouth, and a head shaped more-or-less like ours but they're certainly different.

But I'd become accustomed to Ecostrian faces and she was PRETTY.

"I don't think I can use my mouth on your genitals; the physics just won't work."

"But I think I can do yours and I have a 'toy' you can use on me. I'm certain it would be too large for you."

"But we'll have to wait until we stop for the night."

"I know," she frowned, "but if you would fondle my breasts as we walk, it will help me."

"What about the others?"

"We don't hide such things but if it makes you more comfortable, I'll walk far enough from the group that no one can see clearly."

She went on to explain.

"We Ecostrian females, unlike Humans, are unable to pleasure ourselves properly. While our external genitals are sensitive, we are unable to achieve satisfaction from touching ourselves there. Deep within the vagina is a 'sweet spot' that must be stimulated and it is completely out of reach of the individual. Usually at a rather young age, we learn to have a close female friend help. This is not homosexuality; it is merely helping a friend. Occasionally a pair of young females will form a temporary couple but they quickly separate when males enter the picture. Even into adulthood, when a male is unavailable, we often resort to mutual assistance."

"So now I'm 'one of the girls'?"

"I suppose you could say that. We were shy around you at first and concealed our activities but we've come to accept you."

Because the remainder of the day was very quiet and the night was anything BUT quiet, I'll take a lesson from my husband and invite you to use your own imagination. I'm certainly glad she didn't insist on using that 'toy' on me; I'd have been useless to Human men afterwards. But by the time we were ready to sleep, we were very content.

The next day, Mal'D asked to carry me and I had little doubt what she had in mind for later. Unless we were rescued soon, I was going to 'make the rounds'. I really didn't mind, though; making love with the Ecostrians was a fun change of pace and this way I would get to know each of them much better.

Shortly after mid-day, we came upon a very large river blocking our path.

210

"This leaves little doubt that we're off course." Rala'K fumed. "I remember seeing a large river from the shuttle but it was far south of our base camp."

"What do we do now?" It seemed as if we were all asking the same question.

"About three days ago, we crossed a small stream that I thought could be the one where we first found behortas but it wasn't exactly the same place so we kept going. I believe that if we return to that stream we can follow it to the place where we found behortas on that first day."

"But are we upstream or downstream of the proper location." Was my contribution.

"I'm almost positive that we're upstream from the site we want. I tend to bear left when navigating blind no matter how hard I try to keep a straight course. Let's return to that stream and follow it downstream. If we find nothing after a reasonable time, we can try again in the opposite direction."

So we replenished our water supply and performed an about-face. We could now move more quickly following Rala'K's marked trail but we had about three days of backtracking to accomplish.

The next couple of days passed; if not quickly at the time, there was little to note here. I was carried each day by a different member of the expedition and 'entertained' that night by that person. I'm not going to describe the entertainment but it wasn't at all unpleasant. For anyone who is curious, Ecostrians have a longer, narrower tongue that Humans and the surface is rougher but less rough that that of a cat. In all, a unique and interesting experience.

On the third day of backtracking, we finally came upon the small stream. It did indeed look like the one where we first found behortas but this certainly wasn't the same place.

Han'A was carrying me that day; she insisted that her wounds had healed enough and indeed the wounds were further back than where I would be sitting. Mal'D examined her and pronounced her fit for duty as far as carrying me.

"But if you experience much discomfort, be sure to tell someone. I'm sure we can make arrangements for your night with Free anyway."

"I want to do my part."

"Okay, but don't overdo it."

Traveling downstream was more difficult because we weren't able to choose the terrain; we wanted to keep the stream in sight at all times in order to watch for our original crossing. We knew the spot we wanted would be on the 'left bank' so that's where we traveled.

On the second day of our downstream excursion, we suddenly came upon a waterfall where the little stream dropped over a cliff. The drop was about fifty feet; not a terribly long drop but the cliff face was sheer and none of us was even slightly equipped for mountaineering.

"We can travel along the cliff in one direction or the other; it's bound to have a place where we can get down." Gen'E, my 'mount' for the day, was ever the optimist.

"But it could be a very long distance and take days." Rala'K countered.

"Let's divide into two groups and explore a little in both directions, looking for a way down." I tossed in a couple cents' worth.

"Why not make it three groups? The two food experts can stay here and prepare a meal while the remainder of us look around." Rala'K settled it.

So we split up. Gen'E and I, along with Mal'D headed to the left while the others either went right or set about finding and preparing food.

Patience and dumb luck are often rewarded. We had only traveled about two miles when we found a very large tree that had apparently been blown down by a storm. The upper portion of the tree was extending far out over the cliff while the roots were still anchored in the ground. There were no limbs extending

213

upward from the edge of the cliff for quite some distance. Looking down, we could see that the ground about fifty feet below was firm and fairly level.

"Do we have enough rope to lower people from here?" I was sure we had rope, but was it long enough and strong enough?

"I'm sure we do; Reg'N has a heavy-duty pulley too. But we'll need a harness." Mal'D was helpful.

"I believe that we can reconfigure the straps you use in your packs into a harness." I'd been thinking about that one. "And those large buckles will work a lot like carabiners."

So we made our way back to the stream, where we found meal preparation well underway. It was behorta stew but some of the vegetables and herbs were different so the flavor was unique.

The other exploring party had gone as far as they dared without discovering a way down the cliff. They had returned, discouraged, to the campsite so everyone listened intently while I described my plan.

"We can modify the straps from the packs into a harness to lower each of you by rope using the pulley. The first two or three will be lowered by persons on the cliff above. When there are enough persons below, they can lower the remainder."

214

"What about the equipment?" Rala'K wanted to know.

"We can tie it into as many bundles as necessary and lower it along the way."

"What about you? And how do we get the pulley on and off that tree 'way out there?" The questions were flying.

"All I can see to do is for me to carefully inch my way out on that tree to attach the pulley. After the last of you is lowered, I'll go back out, remove the pulley, and you can lower me by the rope simply over the tree trunk."

"But what if you fall? There won't be anyone to catch you."

"I'll have the rope tied to me. I'll just have to be sure I fall in the direction that has the rope across the tree trunk."

They grudgingly acquiesced; mostly because nobody had a better plan.

Placing the pulley was relatively safe because I could have two ropes, one on each side with a team of friends ready to catch me no matter which way I fell. Even so, inching my way along the large horizontal tree trunk was no piece of cake using only my hands, elbows, and the stumps of my legs.

I was already worried about retrieving the pulley and hoping that Reg'N would decide

215

to abandon it. But it was her property and I wouldn't even suggest such a thing.

We had plenty of very strong rope so we had cut one into shorter pieces to be used in attaching the pulley to the tree trunk. I was never a Girl Scout but I was sure I could do a passable job of tying the pulley to the trunk.

Once the pulley was securely fastened, I passed the longest rope through it then secured it to my safety harness; it would provide added security for my trip back to my friends.

Inching backwards was even more difficult but I finally managed. A couple of times, I nearly fell but managed to maintain my balance. I was very glad to remember that after removing the pulley, I would be descending directly from that spot on the tree trunk.

"Now, how do we do this?" Rala'K was anxious to begin.

"I'm afraid it's going to be scary; a group will hold the long end of the rope while the person to be lowered gets as close as possible to the edge of the cliff then eases over the side. She'll swing back and forth as she is lowered by the ones holding the rope." I could see them all cringe.

"Could a small crew hold another rope to help prevent swinging?" Han'A is no dummy.

"I see no reason why not. If I wasn't so tired, I probably would have thought of that. Once a few people are safely down, we'll lower the equipment then return to lowering people. When most of the people are down, those on the ground will take over the lowering duties."

Being the leader, Rala'K went first. And it was with considerable trepidation she eased herself over the edge of the cliff.

Fortunately, there was a moderately-sized tree in the proper location so the lowering crew could 'belay' the rope around that.

The anti-swing crew eased Rala'K out until the rope was vertical and descent began.

The entire job took most of the day.

Finally, it was only Reg'N and myself remaining on the cliff.

"I'm not sure I can entirely stop you from swinging, but I'll do my best."

"Nonsense. You go down ahead of me and I'll stop you from swinging."

"But there's no way you can go out to recover the pulley."

"You're much more valuable than that pulley. I should have realized that earlier. When I saw you nearly fall coming back in earlier, I decided I didn't want you doing that again."

"If I wasn't so tired, I'd give you a big kiss."

"We can do that later, when you're rested."

"Deal."

By the time everyone was down and we had re-distributed the equipment to the proper people, it was time to call it a night.

Because I had ridden Gen'E briefly at the beginning of the day, she was my 'bunkmate' for the night. We were both, however, too exhausted to do anything more than a sweet goodnight kiss.

The next morning, it was a short walk back to the pool at the base of the waterfall and we resumed our journey downstream.

I know this narrative is becoming rather tedious but I'm editing it from my day-to-day journal. I'm only including the things that seem out of the ordinary and bypassing items such as what we ate on certain days, who I rode, sexual excesses, etc. Trust me, I'm doing the best I can.

Resuming our journey downstream, we were pleased to find food plentiful. Not only were there many behortas in the stream and a large assortment of herbs and vegetables growing along the stream, we saw many herbivorous game animals along the way. Most displayed little fear of us; apparently taking us for fellow herbivores.

"My only problem with all these plant-eaters is that they're bound to attract predators." Ming'R put words to the uneasiness I had been feeling.

"Well, we need to travel near the stream so the only answer is to stay alert and keep our weapons handy." Rala'K answered.

On the 'plus' side, we didn't need to spend much time hunting; when we wanted velocihopper or something similar for dinner, one nearly always appeared. By now, all of us were fairly accurate with both the crossbow and the sling. Field-dressing the more familiar prey was rapid work and only slowed our progress by a few minutes. Suitable herbs and vegetables could be found along our path and we nearly always had more than we needed by the time we stopped for the evening meal. Our survival experts had taught us to make a type of jerky from several different types of game and that, along with fruits and berries gathered *en route,* passed for the noon meal. Our diet wasn't varied but we never went hungry. We still had a sizable store of pre-packaged rations that we had never seen the need to use. We all felt that it might be a good idea to keep them against a time when game might become scarce.

We had been drinking freely from the stream. Originally, we had expected to use water purifiers powered by energy-gathering fields but

219

of course they had stopped working too. In all this time, we just continued drinking untreated water with no ill effects. For my part, I could only hope that I had a natural immunity to the local bacteria and viruses. None of the others became ill either; it was apparently very clean water or very good fortune.

In all, if we weren't badly lost, far from help and out of contact with civilization, this might even have been enjoyable. I would have preferred to have my legs operational so I wasn't a burden on the others but it was sort of fun riding.

"HELP!!"

It was now mid-morning of our second day downstream from the waterfall. I was riding Rala'K for the first time since the new arrangement. I had been wondering if she would expect 'sexual favors' that night. My reverie was shattered by the cry for help.

Shifting into overdrive, Rala'K hurried to the source of the commotion.

We found Reg'N and Ming'R doing battle with an apparition from a nightmare. The others were hurrying to join the battle and I questioned if all of us would be enough.

The creature in question reminded me strongly of an illustration I had once seen on the cover of an Edgar Rice Burroughs novel.

220

This beast was pale and scaly with a huge gaping mouth full of pointed teeth. The creature was shaped rather like an Earthly horned toad but its head was about ten feet above the ground while it probably measured sixty to seventy feet from the snout to the tip of its tail. It had the usual six legs for a denizen of this planet and fortunately it seemed to use all for locomotion but that mouth looked formidable.

I racked my brain for what Burroughs had called this abomination. All I could remember was Great White Lizard. Of course, that was born in the imagination of a writer on Earth in the 1930's and told of an imaginary monster on Mars. It couldn't possibly have anything to do with what we were currently facing. Start thinking in the present, Free!

"Try for its eyes!" Crossbow bolts and large rocks from slings were simply bouncing off the creature's scales and apparently doing no damage.

But my mind kept returning to Barsoom. The hero of the story, I believe his name was Hadron, defeated the creature by throwing a sword into its mouth where it lodged upright between the roof of its mouth and its tongue. That might work here if we had a metal sword or other long sharp metal instrument. I doubted that a crossbow bolt would be long enough or strong enough. My force blade was sort of like a sword but the chances of getting it to lodge between the roof of the lizard's mouth and the tongue were slim and then I would be divesting myself of my most effective weapon.

I needed another option.

Looking around, I spied a cluster of small, straight trees about one and a half to two inches in diameter growing nearby.

"Rala'K, we need to go over to those trees!"

She didn't argue, she just hurried there.

I used my force blade to reach up and cut a straight tree trunk at a sharp angle just below the first branch, forming a very sharp point, then reaching down to cut a downward angle, forming another sharp point. When finished, I had a section of tree trunk about three feet long and two inches in diameter with very sharp points on both ends. We cut five other trees in assorted lengths in the same manner.

Hurrying back to the fray with our booty, we noticed that someone had managed to score a 'hit' on the lizard's left eye with a crossbow bolt. The wound was obviously less than fatal but it hadn't improved the beast's disposition.

I quickly explained my plan to the others.

Reg'N volunteered to try first.

"Be sure to take advantage of that wounded left eye." Rala'K advised. "We'll try to distract it with crossbow fire,"

Reg'N approached the lizard on the left, 'blind', side and attempted to toss a sharpened tree trunk into its mouth in a manner to wedge the mouth open.

But the effort failed. The tree trunk deflected from the creature's teeth and fell to the side. Reg'N attempted to beat a hasty retreat but the lizard saw her with its good eye now.

The huge lizard's tongue shot out and wrapped around Reg'N's waist.

I'm sure the critter normally had better aim but perhaps the damaged eye was at fault.

The tongue was rather narrow and muscular with a large sticky pad at the end. I'm sure it was designed to merely stick to its prey and draw it back but the lizard's depth perception was distorted now.

Now the tongue was hopelessly wrapped around Reg'N and I doubt the lizard could release her even if it wanted.

So the lizard tried to pull her to its mouth.

Ming'R and Gen'E, who were close-by, had other ideas.

So a tug-of-war ensued.

Rala'K and I hurried over and I prepared to slash the tongue with my force blade but stopped at a shout from Mal'D.

"Wait!"

She was standing on the creature's blind side with another of the sharpened tree trunks.

There is little doubt that the lizard was aware of her presence but it couldn't try to snap at her with its tongue extended and with its feet braced for the tug-of-war, it couldn't use them against her.

Almost calmly, she reached into the gaping maw and firmly wedged the sharp tree trunk between the critter's soft palate and tongue. She then hurried away.

"Now cut it!"

I placed my force blade as closely as I dared to Reg'N's body and slashed upwards.

I had no idea a lizard could scream so loudly. It attempted to withdraw its tongue but only got it a short distance when the tree trunk bit too deeply into it's soft palate and the stump of the tongue.

The screaming was now more of a sob as the creature attempted to scuttle backward but was stopped by the small copse of trees and brush it had been using for concealment.

"Are you OK?" I asked Reg'N.

224

"I don't think anything's broken; possibly some bruises." Was the best news I could hope for.

"Rala'K, let's do something about that monster."

So we hurried over to where our former opponent was huddling among the small stand of trees and brush.

Now that I could take time to look at it carefully, it looked a lot like a gigantic gila monster except for the color, which kept changing. When I first saw it, the lizard had been white but now it was rapidly changing to brown, green, grey, mottled dark green, and several other shades.

I had no doubt now that this was an ambush predator; doing its business from the concealment of brush and small stands of trees; changing color to blend in. The creature would use its long sticky tongue to capture small to medium-sized prey like velocihoppers. It wasn't equipped to fight anything as large and well equipped as us but the battle had been forced upon it.

I was beginning to feel sorry for it. There was no possibility of it's recovery from the wounds we had inflicted. The future for it would only be pain and death.

"Rala'K, take me close to it; I want to end it's misery."

"And that confounded shrieking."

"That, too."

So she took me close to it's left side where I used my force blade to sever the spine just behind the skull. The lizard shuddered a couple times, the color changing stopped, and it stopped breathing.

This creature only bore a superficial resemblance to the one described by Edgar Rice Burroughs. His lizard was white all the time and didn't have the long tongue. And his lizard reportedly had purple blood that carried a foul odor. This one had red blood and while I wouldn't choose it as a perfume scent, the odor wasn't worse than any other blood.

All sense of victory for me vanished. Sure, we had triumphed over a dangerous opponent but had it really been necessary to fight at all? I discussed the point with Rala'K as we made our way back to the others.

When we got back, Mal'D was tending to Reg'N's injuries while the others were gathering up scattered crossbow bolts and equipment.

"Ladies, we need a meeting!" Rala'K called loudly. The others gathered 'round.

"First of all, how is Reg'N?"

Both Reg'N and Mal'D assured her that the injuries were minimal and Reg'N would be able to continue when the others were ready.

"Very good. That was a brave act, attempting to wedge that stump in the creature's mouth. That tongue surprised us all and everyone improvised well on the response. In all, I'm very pleased with the teamwork everyone displayed in this battle. There was no time to give detailed instructions; everyone just did what needed to be done."

"However, Free mentioned an important point: Did we really need to fight that thing at all? Once we knew where it was, why didn't we just avoid it? The lizard was too slow to chase us and it wasn't capable of eating us so it wasn't interested. We only fought and killed it because it was different and, to our eyes, ugly."

"We need to develop a policy of only fighting and risking our lives when necessary. A creature like that one presents no threat to us once we know where it is and we can avoid it. From now on, we'll just avoid opponents when we can. We could easily have lost Reg'N today just to fight a creature that presented no threat to us. Let us remember, we're here to survive, not conquer a world."

When she finished speaking, everyone was quiet for a few moments then a murmur of assent began.

"You're right, Rala'K, we just got caught up in the moment but fighting that thing was foolish." Was the general tone of the response.

"But now, I'd like to move some distance downstream before we camp for the night. I don't want to be too close to that body because it could attract a lot of scavengers. Let's move a few miles then we'll get some rest."

Equipment was re-distributed to the proper persons and stowed for traveling. We were only able to recover thirty-seven crossbow bolts after this battle; the craftspeople had been spending their evenings making bolts and the count before now was sixty-six but we all considered this a small loss. The remaining bolts were distributed as evenly as possible.

Once again, we set out downstream.

But this time we had only progressed a couple of miles when Gen'E, who was on 'point', sent word back for Rala'K to hurry to the front.

"You need to see this." She greeted Rala'K.

She indicated a pile of behorta shells. Seeing this and looking around, I realized that this was the place where we had first been introduced to behortas at the beginning of this odyssey. We were only a short march from base camp!

228

The remainder of the group, when they arrived, all agreed.

"It's too late in the day to go there now. Let's make camp here and finish the trip in the morning." Rala'K has a whim of iron.

It made good sense, though, Reg'N was obviously sore and everyone was tired from the battle. In the excitement, none of us had eaten since early in the day. We should camp, get cleaned up, eat, and get a good night's rest.

Ming'R and Gen'E had each shot and field dressed velocihoppers while most of the others had been collecting vegetables and herbs along the way so it was a simple matter to put together a delicious stew that evening. I would, however, have given anything for a plate of Kirk's sauerbraten und spätzle.

The local fare was quite good but I needed a change of pace. Come to think of it, an ice-cold draft beer sounded terribly good too.

Surprisingly, Rala'K wanted to make love that night and she was very tender and loving. As I explained before, Ecostrian females are physically incapable of giving themselves pleasure so they usually 'pair off' temporarily for such pursuits. This isn't like human homosexuality or bisexuality because most Ecostrian female pairings are brief and easily stopped when a suitable male becomes available. In out group, the others had been switching around, not generally staying with the same partners two nights in a row but Rala'K had held herself aloof; feeling that the leader shouldn't become involved.

Therefore, she was very frustrated and 'pent up'.

I had been with all the others many times so I knew exactly what to do. Rala'K's release, when it came, nearly woke the entire camp.

"So much for discretion, But I'm sure the others are happy for you." I assured her.

"Do you think so?"

"Of course. They all like you and I'm sure any of them would be happy to be where I am right now."

An Ecostrian smile isn't quite like a human smile but it's very pretty once you get accustomed to it.

"Now, how do I please you?"

I had to teach her but once she learned what to do, she liked what she was doing and she was very good at it. I'm sure I wasn't as loud as she but it certainly felt good. 'Nuff said.

The next day, I was scheduled to ride Reg'N but she begged off, saying she felt that she was up to traveling but carrying my extra weight could be too much. Rala'K was happy to volunteer for the 'double shift'. I saw some sly grins on the faces of the others but I'm sure there was no ill will. They felt that Rala'K deserved it.

Now the walk felt familiar. All along the path we saw things we remembered from our first day on this trip. Rala'K had to keep reminding everyone to maintain constant vigilance; now we had a better idea of the dangers of this area.

"And we don't know the food situation at base camp. We might as well hunt along the way." She reminded us.

Anticipation was running high. Despite repeated reminders, most of the ladies seemed to feel that all our troubles would be solved when we reached base camp. Rala'K tried to reign in their enthusiasm.

"Remember, it's very unlikely that they have power either and they might not even have hunting equipment as good as ours."

Han'A was on point when she sent back word for Rala'K to come to the front.

This was much worse than even the most pessimistic of us could have imagined.

Of the four shuttles that had formed our base camp, one was now lying on its back and completely destroyed with the main access door torn open. Another was rightside-up but the door was ripped out with a large gaping hole in its place. The other two were apparently intact but there was no sign of occupancy and the ground in the immediate vicinity showed signs of a considerable disturbance; small trees were broken and the tripods that the base camp crew had erected for cooking were lying on the ground. No persons were evident.

"Something or someone attacked the camp. We need to investigate but whomever or whatever did this could still be out there. Han'A and Mal'D, please stand guard while the rest of us investigate." Rala'K was being cautious.

Inside one of the intact shuttles we found a note in the Ecostrian language.

The translators provided by the Arisians do a fine job of translating spoken words but they are absolutely no help with writing.

"What does it say?"

Rala'K translated without comment or editorializing:

"RalaK,

If you find this, we had to abandon the shuttles and take refuge in a cave we found about three miles north of here. We marked trees along the way by removing large pieces of bark.

All of our powered equipment has failed and we are unable to call for assistance. The shuttles have no power. The night after you left, the camp was attacked by a very big creature. This monster overturned one of the shuttles and ripped the access door from it. After that, it was able to reach inside and remove the persons inside and eat them.

The next night, the monster returned and removed the door from another shuttle after which it ate the crew of that shuttle.

Given the circumstances, we felt that we must abandon the camp for the cave we had found while exploring. The cave is large enough to shelter us but too small for the monster to enter.

We have no weapons that can possibly harm this immense creature but we hope to devise methods of obtaining food.

Please come to us when you return from your exploration.

Min'E"

"This is terrible. How many were in each shuttle crew?"

"Each shuttle had a crew of two persons." Rala'K replied.

"So that's four dead."

"And hopefully four still alive at the cave. We'll have to go there and help them as soon as possible. I only wonder what kind of monster we face now."

"Min'E didn't describe it at all so we're still in for a surprise.

So we set out for the cave and now everyone was at full alert. Not only were we watching for an unknown huge monster, we were hoping to add as much as possible to the food supply.

The 'basic training' we had all experienced over the last few days had prepared us well for this walk. The group acted as a well-trained team, covering each other with unconscious teamwork. No one made a move without being covered by one or two others.

By the time our trail led us to a narrow canyon, we had collected two velocihoppers along with a considerable assortment of herbs and vegetables and three behortas. No unknown monsters, however.

Nearing the end of the canyon, we found a small cave opening and at the cave mouth we saw a fire burning.

Tending the fire was the co-pilot of the lead shuttle.

"I'm certainly happy to see you. Let me get Min'E."

She hurried into the cave and quickly returned with Min'E

It wasn't an overly emotional reunion because the exploratory party and shuttle crews didn't know each other well but all were happy to see each other.

"We found your note. Can you give us more details about what happened?"

"The creature attacked and while we were trying to decide what to do, all of our electronic equipment stopped working so we couldn't call for help or even fly away."

"How did you find this place?"

"It was obvious that we were going to be here for a long time so a couple of the girls went hunting. They found this place and it's a good thing they did. That monster proved that the shuttles are no refuge from it."

"Why do you have a fire burning on such a warm day?"

"The monster seems to be afraid of fire and with even the daytime hours so dark, fire is effective all the time."

"It must keep you busy, collecting wood along with food."

"Indeed it does but we have little else to do. We managed to make simple bows and arrows for hunting but they're of little use against the monster. When it appears, all we can do is run or hide."

"What is this monster like?" I was really curious.

"It's like nothing we've ever seen before. It has a scaly green skin and four walking legs. It has an upright forward torso similar to us but its head is much larger in proportion to its body. The head is elongated with a huge, toothy mouth. It has long arms with claws that seem very good at grasping prey. The creature itself is several times larger than any of us and it is obviously predatory. When it first attacked our base camp, it overturned one shuttle then managed to rip the door completely from the hull. It then reached in and dragged out the crew before eating them. It must have enjoyed the taste because it came back the next evening and went straight to the next shuttle where it simply ripped off the door, dragged out the crew, and ate them. After that, we decided that the shuttles were no refuge so we moved here. However, the monster has somehow followed us here and appears every evening. It prowls around for several hours and we're certain that only our fire and the small cave entrance keep it out. Our arrows and thrown rocks have no effect upon it. Eventually it goes away, apparently in search of other food."

"Well, I doubt that our crossbows or slings will do much to stop this thing either. And it sounds too dangerous to ignore. We need to find some way to fight it. I want to see it when it appears tonight but in the mean time, I'll look around and see if I can come up with any ideas."

Min'E carried me around the area for a 'tour of inspection'. I hoped this didn't mean I would owe her any sexual favors but kept my mouth shut, hoping for the best.

The interior of the cave was much larger than I had expected with a large expanse of level floor and a high, domed ceiling. Near the back was a spring with a pool of water that somehow had an outlet to the outside because the water was kept fresh.

"What are all those yellow streaks in the rocks?"

"Mil'A studied geology and she tells me that it's sulphur. Apparently it's a very common mineral here." I filed that away in my head as possibly useful data.

She showed me around the remainder of the area, including the approach to the cave entrance. I had been so focused of getting here that the terrain hadn't really registered. Now I was paying close attention

The cave was at the end of a narrow rocky split in the ground. The 'floor' of this split was relatively level and the split narrowed near the cave end. Just outside the cave entrance the split was barely twenty feet in width with uneven walls on both sides. Close examination led to the discovery of a mini-cave about fifty feet from the cave entrance and about four feet above the valley floor. The mini-cave would barely hold an Ecostrian and would be difficult for one to enter in a hurry but I was beginning to have another idea for it. Now, if I could only gather all the materials I needed.

"Min'E, I have an idea but it requires a lot of things we don't have. It's possible we can make them but it will take everyone working together."

"Perhaps we should call a meeting and ask everyone what they can do."

I won't go into the details of the meeting but it wound up with Ming'R and Gen'E each in charge of a 'task force' that would be manufacturing materials for my project. Rala'K and Min'E would both help me with the remaining part.

By now, it was nearly time for the monster to make its usual visit.

It failed to disappoint. The creature appeared just beyond the limits of the fire that had been built up just for the occasion.

This critter made me think of a compilation of a tyrannosaurus rex and an apatosaurus, It had a heavy body with four walking legs much like the apatosaurus but forward of the front walking legs, the tyrannosaurus took over. The upright torso led up to a pair of arms much longer in proportion to its body than a t rex and equipped with some nasty-looking grasping claws.

But the scariest part was its head. At about thirty feet above the ground, it was the part that most resembled our old friend t-rex with the gaping toothy mouth and the small beady eyes. And somehow I could sense a crafty intelligence in this creature; it wouldn't be easy to outwit.

As usual, the monster spent some time hanging around hoping for a way into the cave and eventually went in search of easier prey.

"You're right; we're not safe here with that thing running loose. We'll have to kill it."

"We never see it in the daytime so that will be the best time for us to gather our materials and work on our projects."

"And first thing tomorrow will be the time to start. These projects will take several days and we won't be safe until that thing is dead."

Our projects necessarily began with a trip back to the shuttles for supplies. Ming'R needed a large, porous cloth and the privacy curtain from one of the wrecked shuttles should do nicely.

Gen'E needed a couple of things:

She selected an item that looked a lot like an Earthly chain saw along with two containers that looked much like heavily-built two-gallon gasoline containers and some shovels that appeared to be much like the ones used on Earth and two large sheets of heat-resistant plastic.

"This fuel container is nearly empty. These saws are part of the shuttles' survival equipment and the fuel containers should always be full. I had to get another from the shuttle that was turned over."

"What fuel does the saw use?"

"This is one place where we had an advantage over Earth even before outsiders brought energy-gathering fields. We have a mineral that burns cleanly without harmful emissions. This is that mineral ground into a fine powder. It will power the saw and the only exhaust will be water vapor and carbon dioxide. We used this mineral to power most industry and vehicles for many generations without the problems Earth had by using hydrocarbons."

"Can we use that powdered mineral as an explosive?"

"I'm afraid not. It's not explosive and that's normally a good thing. In order to power an internal combustion engine, a small amount must first be ignited and used to heat another metered quantity. That heated mineral gives off a gas that then becomes explosive and will power the engine. The only way to use it as an explosive would be to have a large fire and a chamber collecting a quantity of gas before detonating it."

"So you've had clean, safe energy for many generations."

"Yes, and we were spared the pollution troubles Earth faced until your friend Scott Montgomery discovered energy-gathering fields,"

"It's too bad Earth doesn't have that mineral. We could have saved a lot of grief."

"The mineral is very common on our planet and easily obtained. We only need to mill it into a powder to use it as a power source for internal combustion engines. In the bulk form, it can be burned to power steam turbines or simple home heating equipment. No matter how it's used, there are no harmful emissions other than carbon dioxide and water vapor."

"Do you have hydrocarbons here?"

"We have discovered some petroleum and refine a small amount to be used as lubricants and in manufacturing but we've never needed to use it as fuel. That has kept our environment very clean."

"And I've noticed that much more of your planet has forest and vegetation. That must help convert all the extra carbon dioxide back into oxygen."

"Yes; Ecostria has a much smaller population than Earth so much more of the surface is left to grow naturally. Also, we've never been a seafaring race so our oceans are almost completely unexplored and unspoiled. Few people realize how much atmosphere is processed by an ocean."

"So your race evolved on only one continent?"

"Yes; we didn't colonize the other land masses until after the discovery of anti-gravity transportation that allowed us to travel over the bodies of water. After that, it was a simple matter to spread over the northern hemisphere. We never did, however, care to explore south of the Great Rift until this expedition. I believe it was mostly rumor and superstition but stories abounded of dire fates befalling anyone who came here."

"Of course, we hadn't been here long before things started going wrong."

"I still believe we can make it out of here and prove the superstitions wrong. We merely need to keep trying."

"With that in mind, we should get our new equipment back to the cave so we can start the projects tomorrow."

"Agreed; let's go."

Before we left, I selected a few items that I thought would be useful: a half-dozen lighting fixtures from the destroyed shuttles that were essentially thin plastic tubes about six inches in length and sealed on one end with a low-voltage bulb at the other end. These were in various colors but color didn't matter to me. I then selected a long roll of two-conductor wire, probably about sixteen gauge and I would guess about one hundred feet long along with two large electrical storage batteries that had been the emergency power supplies for the wrecked shuttles.

By the time we had lugged all this plunder back to the cave it was getting fairly late.

Our 'friend', whom I nicknamed Rex, made his usual appearance that evening to remind us of the reason for all this activity. While I'm sure we could have tried running away, he could easily have followed us and our next refuge might not be as secure as this one. We all felt that our present location was the best place to stand and fight.

Now to prepare for the fight.

Ming'R began her task by carefully cleaning a large area of the cave floor where there was a shallow depression. It appeared to me that the area would form a pool of water if it ever became wet but that didn't seem to worry Ming'R. After the initial cleaning, she used a tree branch much like a pine bough to carefully sweep the area of as much dust as possible. After that she spread the large porous privacy curtain from the wrecked shuttle on the floor.

She then gathered her crew and they left in search of materials.

In the mean time, Gen'E and her crew were cutting wood. She had noticed a couple dead trees along the path between the cave and the shuttles and she said they were the precise species of tree that she wanted. They found it simpler to cut the wood to size at the site then bring it back in pieces.

"When that fuel can is empty, be sure to bring it to me; I have plans for it." I told her.

While most of the people were gone, Min'E, Rala'K, and I began our task.

We harvested as much yellow mineral as we could from the walls and ceiling of the cave then used very hard stones to grind it into a fine powder. It was back-breaking labor and I crushed my fingers many times but by the end of the day we had amassed a sizable supply of powdered sulphur.

While we were doing this, Ming'R and her people came in toting large bundles of plants and two bags of leaves made from those sheets of plastic taken from the shuttles. Those were all piled on the cloth that had been arranged on the floor.

"Ming'R, I've read about how this is done on Earth and I never saw anything about this. What are you doing?" I just had to ask.

"We use potassium nitrate as a food preservative and this is the quickest method. There are several other ways but they can require up to a year and use materials we don't have. Here, we have y'barra plants which have a very high potassium content and mucolla leaves which are rich in nitrogen. We'll pile them all together then simply walk on them until they're reduced as much as possible to powder. After that, we sprinkle them with a small amount of water to wash the powder from the large solid pieces then pull up the cloth, leaving a thick liquid that is rich in potassium nitrate. After that, we simply let the water evaporate, leaving behind powdered potassium nitrate."

"And you're certain that this will work?"

"I've done it many times to preserve meat. I was thinking of making some anyway if we were going to be here for a long time."

"How much do you expect to make this time?"

"This batch should produce a pile of powder about the same size as that pile of yellow mineral you have over there."

"How long will it take?"

"It depends on the humidity and air circulation but I expect it to be four to five days."

"I don't expect the other materials to be ready any sooner so that should work out fine."

I turned to Rala'K. "And speaking of the other materials, will you take me outside so we can see how Gen'E and her crew are doing?"

Outside, we found Gen'E and her group had returned with bundles of cut and split hard wood about two feet long. They were now busily digging two pits and arranging the lengths of wood into teepee shapes in the pits.

"I've read about this process but I've never seen it done."

"What we do is make the hard wood into cone shapes then cover them tightly with dirt. Then we'll cover that with those heat-resistant plastic sheets to keep most of the air out. After that, we'll start a very 'slow' fire in the center of each cone and allow it to burn very slowly for several days. This will dry and char the hard wood without actually consuming it. When we're done, what remains is called charcoal."

"Awesome! It sounds as if you've done this before."

"My father was in the business of making charcoal for most of his life. I helped him a lot as a small child. Of course, he used a large manufacturing plant but the principle is the same."

"How long do you expect this to take?"

"The industry standard is five days and if we can light our fires today, I believe we can have charcoal ready to use in five days."

So now we merely needed to tend our projects and stay alive for a few days. Ming'R and her people trampled the vegetable matter into a fine dust, sprinkled it with water, and pulled up the cloth, leaving a thick slurry in the shallow depression in the floor. Ming'R assured me that it would dry into exactly what I wanted.

Gen'E spent a lot of time tending her 'kilns', making sure that no excess air was entering to accelerate the burn.

In the mean time the others hunted, ate, explored a little, slept, made love, and generally led an idyllic life.

I, on the other hand, spent a lot of time worrying about my husband, Kirk. I hadn't expected to be away this long without at least checking in with him. When I left, he was having the time of his life with that around-the-clock orgy but even he would have to get tired of that eventually. But there was nothing I could do until I found my way out of this current mess.

"One step at a time, Free."

Our friend Rex continued to visit every evening and added a nightly serenade. I have no idea what he thought he was doing; perhaps he was trying to invite us to come out and play. He certainly didn't have a good singing voice and even a full orchestra behind him wouldn't have been much help. Fortunately he didn't seem to have a long attention span and he would wander off after a couple hours.

The 'pool' was getting drier every day. I could see that it would be a powder very soon. Fortunately there were no gusts of wind in the cave or we could have lost a lot of our hard-earned material.

Likewise, Gen'E reported that the charcoal was nearly ready. She was going to add more oxygen-robbing material to completely snuff the internal fires and finish the process. Once the fires were extinguished, we would have charcoal; perhaps not as neat as commercial briquettes but it should do nicely for our purposes.

Now how to mix the final product? I knew the proper ingredients but how much of each? I decided the thing to do was start my experiments with small but equal amounts of each ingredient and see how that worked. After that, I'd vary the amounts of each and see what worked best. Once I arrived at the optimum mixture, I'd concoct as much of the final product as possible and we'd build our device.

The potassium nitrate was ready. It was in the form of a fine grey-white powder and should mix nicely.

The charcoal was exhumed and allowed to cool then scraped into a fine grey-black powder.

So now I had three piles of powder; yellow, grey-white, and black. Each pile was about the size of a two-gallon bucket and if I managed to make it all into the substance I wanted, it should be more than enough.

I started by taking about a teaspoon full of each substance and mixing them together. After that I had Rala'K carry me outside and away from the cave entrance. I carefully poured the mixture on an area of bare rock then ignited it with an Ecostrian match.

The results were much more spectacular than I had expected. There was a bright flash and a 'poof!' A large cloud of grey-black smoke drifted away on the breeze. I had created black powder on my first attempt even though it wasn't really black.

For my next experiment, I used one of the lighting fixtures from the wrecked shuttle.

I opened the plastic tube and removed the low voltage light bulb. I broke the glass bulb while being careful not to damage the filament inside. Then I lightly filled the plastic fixture with my black powder before replacing the broken bulb. I attached one end of the one hundred foot spool of wire to the fixture then had Rala'K carry me what we both considered to be a safe distance away before connecting one conductor of the wire to a battery.

I sat on the ground, prepared to touch the other conductor to the battery.

"Are we ready for this?" I asked Rala'K

"I hope so."

It wasn't an Earth-shattering explosion. It wasn't even an Ecostria-shattering explosion. But it was a rather large and satisfying explosion considering the relatively small amount of powder used and the lack of proper containment.

And this had only been a prototype blasting cap.

Back in the cave, I mixed all the powder then constructed two more blasting caps. I then placed the blasting caps in the bottom of the fuel can and filled it with black powder. The wires from the blasting caps were run up through the pouring spout and wired in parallel so that if one failed the other would still function.

I had my IED, or Improvised Explosive Device.

Now we needed to place it where it would do us the most good.

It was too late in the day to begin the next phase so I spent a restless night second-guessing myself.

The next day, all of us headed for the mini-cave along the approach to our fortress.

We placed the IED at the rear of the mini-cave and attached the wires carefully to the long roll of wire which was then arranged as discretely as possible along the route back into our cave.

After that, we began filling the mini-cave loosely with small to medium-sized rocks. These would take the place of shrapnel in a more conventional bomb.

The mini-cave itself had become something like a civil war mortar.

When finished, it would not have attracted attention or stood out as a thing of beauty. It did, however, represent the work of many days on our part and the hopes of all of us.

Now we were looking forward to Rex's next visit.

Sitting in the cave entrance, I realized that there was a major flaw in the plan; I couldn't see the mini-cave from where I was sitting, If someone were to wait outside watching for Rex, it would probably cause him to hurry too quickly past the mini-cave for me to have a chance to detonate the IED at the proper time.

"All we can do is to wait through another of his visits. Then, after he turns to leave, someone will sneak out behind him and signal you when he's near the cave." Rala'K has a good head on her shoulders.

No clandestine lover has ever been more eagerly anticipated than Rex was that evening. I actually enjoyed his serenade but of course was anxious for it to end.

Rex finally 'sang' his last note then stood staring at the cave, perhaps hoping one or more of us would succumb to his call. When none of us came out, he turned to leave.

Min'E, being the smallest and fastest, had been picked to shadow Rex. She gave him a reasonable head start then slipped quietly from our cave.

She only needed to go as far as the first large boulder that was obstructing my view from our cave entrance. From there she could see everything she needed.

Almost immediately upon reaching the boulder, she signaled me. Rex was at the mini-cave.

I hurriedly touched the bare wire to the battery post and was rewarded by a roar much louder than I had expected. It sounded as if I had touched off the end of the world.

Min'E stood there, staring around the boulder.

Rala'K called to her.

"Min'E, did it work?"

"Oh, it worked, all right. Rex is no longer a threat but we might need to dig out way out of here!"

It wasn't really that bad. Rex had been converted into a large hunk of shredded meat and pushed against the far wall of the little canyon. The wall of the canyon that had held the mini-cave had been blasted into gravel and larger chunks of rock had cascaded down, covering the floor of the canyon and half-burying Rex.

We found that by moving some of the larger rocks, it was possible to clamber over the obstruction to reach the other side.

With Rex no longer a threat we could now return to the shuttles. Removing Rex's corpse would be quite a job and with it in place, that vicinity was going to become extremely malodorous for quite some time.

It was only about a three mile hike back to our original base camp. We were encumbered by a lot of equipment we had taken to the cave but managed to haul it in one trip after I taught the others how to make the travois I'd once seen in a movie.

When we sighted base camp, we were greeted by a pleasant surprise.

Along with the Ecostrian shuttles were three Star Fleet shuttles and several persons in Star Fleet uniforms!

As we hurried into camp, I saw that one of the persons present was my brother-in-law, Scott Montgomery.

"Scotty! What are you doing here?"

"Looking for you, of course. Where have you been?"

"It's a long story but all of our powered equipment failed, including my legs and then we got lost. We've been wandering around in this forest fighting strange creatures most of the time."

"I know about the equipment failure; it was caused by a volcano eruption that filled the atmosphere with a strange cloud of gas that somehow screened reception of energy to the field generators. It's taken this long to dissipate. We knew we'd lost contact with you but we couldn't even bring the *Enterprise* here to look."

"Where's Kirk?"

His face lost the customary smile.

"That's another reason we weren't searching as much as we normally would. There's bad news about Kirk."

I must have looked panicked because he hurried on.

"He's still alive but he had a bad heart attack shortly after you left. You were already out of contact so his brother, Dick, and I became his next-of-kin to make decisions. This is where things get complicated. He's alive and nothing irreversible has been done so far. Maybe you should see him and talk to him before anything is done then let Doctor de Beers and me explain what we want to do."

"Who is this Dr de Beers?"

"He's a medical researcher from Earth who had come to Arisia to show me something he's been developing. By a great stroke of good fortune, what he's been developing could be exactly what's going to save Kirk."

"Let's go."

"I guess the first thing you should do is get into the shuttle and grab a shower. After that, I brought you another spare set of legs and these have a battery back-up, just in case. Your old ones should be working now but we won't take any chances. I brought you a Star Fleet uniform, too. These three shuttles are the ones we used in the Andromeda Galaxy some time ago and they're the ones with beefed-up battery back-ups too."

So Scotty helped me into the shower. After all this time bathing in creeks without soap, a real shower would have felt great but I was too worried about Kirk to truly enjoy it. Having legs again was a considerable relief though.

I said my hurried goodbyes to my fellow castaways and promised to be in touch when my present emergency was resolved.

On our flight back north, Scotty filled me in:

"Kirk was partying his tush off just as you might expect and apparently he just overstrained his heart. Fortunately, Easy was present at the time and she used that mind power she got from the Arachna to keep him alive while someone called for medical assistance. But when they examined him, they found that his heart was terribly damaged. They've had him

249

on full life support since it happened and were considering a heart transplant. However, it seems that a transplant is terribly complicated by his diabetes; it seems that his refusal to properly care for his diabetes probably had a lot to do with this heart attack. So now, we arranged to meet a Medoo hospital ship here on Ecostria because they have better life support equipment. The word is that no one has ever died while under Medoo care. But the Medoo tell me that they can only support him, not cure him. However, Dr. du Beers was visiting from Earth to show me a revolutionary artificial heart he's been developing. His device uses my field, both for power and to impel the blood.

"So now you want to put this experimental unit into Kirk?"

"The one he brought was a cut-away model, for demonstration only. The device hasn't been approved by the FDA for manufacture or use on human beings yet but of course we're far outside the jurisdiction of the FDA here. Dick and I discussed it and you weren't available. We decided to go ahead but now that you're here, you'll have the final word but it seems to be the best chance Kirk has."

"If the one he brought couldn't be used, what were you going to do?"

"One of my medical equipment factories is ready to start producing these things as soon as they get approval. In fact, I had them make two, just in case. Starship *Freedom Seven* was on Earth for some minor repairs and they are currently enroute to Ecostria carrying those two artificial hearts."

"Why two?"

"I just don't trust new technology with something as important as Kirk's life. The Enterprisian Star Cluster has a tried-and true

250

implantable switching valve that can mate with the hearts. Starship *Leonard Wood* was near Enterprisia so she is enroute with that system as we speak. The Arisians are growing and programming a molecular computer that will control the entire system. The doctors will implant both artificial hearts in Kirk and each will do half the work even though one would be more than enough to do the job. If either fails, the computer will shut it down and the other heart will take over the job while the computer sends a trouble alert. Research ship *Sacajawea* is bringing the computer control system from Arisia and the surgery will take place aboard the Medoo ship. But this all hinges on your consent."

"Is Kirk conscious?"

"He wasn't able to talk when we got him to Ecostria but the Medoo doctors told me they were certain he would be very much improved after their life support equipment had time to stabilize him. However, in order to remain stable, he must stay in their bed and connected to the equipment."

"So it's not a long-term solution."

"Right. They can keep him alive almost forever—if he stays in their bed. But we both know how happy he'll be about that. I've looked around and asked my medical experts. Everyone I've talked to thinks Dr. du Beers has the best answer."

"Just wait til I get Kirk home."

"Yeah, there need to be a lot of changes made."

"Will he need to stop swinging?"

"Not necessarily. Dr. du Beers tells me that this new heart system should be stronger and more dependable than any human heart. But Kirk will need to control his diabetes. The next body system to go may be even more difficult to replace than his heart."

"I don't know much about diabetes and Kirk never discusses it."

"We'll get a Certified Diabetes Educator or an Endocrinologist here to lay down the law for Kirk but let me give you what I managed to learn from my studies:

A human body is made up of trillions of cells, nerve, muscle, bone, etc. and each of those cells needs food. The body supplies that food by converting what we eat into a simple sugar called glucose. Of course, there are vitamins, amino acids, minerals, etc. but right now we're dealing with the glucose. Now, the glucose is released into the blood stream where it circulates around the body to be absorbed into the cells in order to nourish them. Now to avoid over feeding the cells, there's a control system that only allows a certain amount of glucose into each cell then shuts off the supply. To regulate that system, we have an organ called the pancreas. The pancreas measures the amount of glucose in the blood and secretes a hormone called insulin that unlocks the cells to allow glucose into them. A person with diabetes has a breakdown of that insulin system. Either the pancreas isn't secreting insulin or the insulin isn't working. When that happens, glucose builds up in the blood but the cells are starving to death anyway. In Kirk's case, the heart muscles starved so much that too many of them died. In many cases, the nerve cells are affected first and the patient has neurological trouble."

"So even if we get Kirk past this crisis, he needs to get the diabetes under control."

"Absolutely. It's totally a matter of life and death. He could have a stroke next and as far as I know, nobody is working on an artificial brain."

I was stunned. Kirk had seldom mentioned his diabetes and rarely did anything about it. He had a glucose test meter somewhere in the dresser drawer and occasionally tested his blood but he never stuck with any kind of diet. On a couple occasions, I heard him say: 'I'm not supposed to eat that because I'm diabetic.' But then he'd usually eat it anyway. I always thought he was joking. As the kids say: My Bad.

My first instinct was to march in and read him the riot act but that would be bad form with a man who's on life support. Besides that, I knew just as soon as I saw him I was going to break down into tears. I needed to control that too.

Try to think happy thoughts, Free. What had Scotty said? Oh, yeah, *Freedom Seven* would be bringing that control valve from Enterprisia. That meant our son, Patrick. I hadn't seen him in a long time and I was sure I could talk Star Fleet into allowing him to stay until after the surgery.

And the *Leonard Wood* meant Captain John McCoy, who'd trained under Kirk aboard the *Enterprise* and earned his own ship. He was such a nice, competent young man and I'd be happy to see him. The *Sacajawea* meant the nice Captain Tammy Anderson who had been awarded her own starship but hadn't made it to Earth yet to get it.

So when the shuttle landed alongside the Medoo ship *Mother of Mercy,* I was showered, dressed in regulation Star Fleet uniform, and walking on my own two legs.

We were quickly introduced to Dr. Perla, who was in charge of Kirk's case.

"Ah, yes. Admiral James is in fine condition now. He's fully conscious and able to converse. He's been asking about you, Commander James, but I didn't know what to tell him. He does know that he can't leave the life support bed until after surgery but we haven't explained the surgery to him yet."

"What is your opinion of this surgical option, Doctor?" I just had to ask.

"Usually in a case like this we try to obtain a cadaver transplant but that is enormously complicated by his endocrine disorder. I have reviewed the data on the proposed implant and it looks very good. The proposal to implant two units is perhaps excessive but almost certain to guarantee success."

"So you approve?"

"It is far better than anything we can do for him at our current level of technology."

"Do you know Doctor du Beers?"

"I have met him and shown him our facilities. He will be using our operating suite assisted by our staff and a human assistant of his choice. I will also be present and available for consultation if I may be of any assistance."

"Before I make my final decision, I suppose I should talk to Kirk; after all, it is his life we're talking about."

"I completely agree and it might be a good idea to have Doctor du Beers present also to explain exactly what he wants to do as well as show both of you the demonstration model of the artificial heart."

****

"I'm very pleased to meet you, Commander James. I haven't had the chance to examine Admiral James yet but I've studied his medical history and case files very carefully. I'm certain we can help him."

"But you look so young, Doctor."

"Yes, I am young, Commander, and the admiral will be my first actual patient since graduating medical school. But in my own defense, I went directly from school into research on this artificial heart and it has been my sole occupation for several years. Now that it's finally ready, I feel compelled to be the first to implant it."

"I do hope you're a qualified surgeon."

"Indeed I am. I graduated at the top of my class at Harvard Medical in cardiology and was offered a partnership in a prestigious practice but I had my sights set on research; I had for many years been planning this artificial heart but I needed the medical degree first so I got it."

"And you'll have expert Medoo doctors there to assist if you need them?"

"Along with a human doctor. I haven't chosen one yet but there are several fine surgeons available among the assembled starships present."

"How did you manage to go so quickly from medical school into such intense research?"

"A classmate of mine had a father who was a rather influential thoracic surgeon and he was impressed by my plans for the artificial heart. He spoke to some of his friends and one was connected with the Montgomery Foundation for Medical Advancement. After graduation, I was contacted by a representative and after jumping through a lot of hoops, I was swimming in grant money and technical assistance. When I published my findings, I was emailed directly by Mister Montgomery and invited to visit him aboard the *Enterprise*. I hopped aboard a supply shuttle and arrived just after Admiral James had suffered this myocardial infarction."

"So the timing couldn't have worked out any more perfectly."

"To be honest, I would have preferred to have obtained FDA approval before implanting the first unit but I'm confident that my unit will perform as designed. Mister Montgomery insists on using two and that will make doubly certain of success but one should be more than enough."

"What happens if one of the units does develop a problem?"

"If that does happen, the Arisian computer will cut that unit out of the system and the other unit will assume the entire load while the computer sends a signal to me and all Star Fleet medical facilities informing us of the problem. At that point, we'll probably make a decision to replace the faulty unit as quickly as possible."

"So he'll be safer with this unit than with his natural heart?"

"Let me put it this way: he won't be immortal but he certainly won't die of a heart attack. I can guarantee that."

"Is there a 'downside' to this?"

"All I can think of is the fact that these hearts move the blood using a constant, steady flow. That means that he won't have a pulse and conventional blood pressure measurements won't operate because there won't be a systolic or diastolic to measure. My system has very precise pressure measuring equipment in the aorta and vena cava and those readings, along with other vital signs, will be available for readout on a special wristwatch he'll need to wear along with a larger unit I'll supply to Star Fleet Medical. Those readings, along with other

256

critical vital medical information, will be available to his doctors and me by telemetry at any time we care to check."

"So you and other doctors will be watching over him for the rest of his life?"

"In a manner of speaking. We won't be able to see what he's doing or hear what he's saying; he'll have total privacy. But at the first sign of a medical problem, all of us will be aware of it."

"I can't ask for better than that, unless a doctor could be with him constantly."

"And even that has its occasional downside; often a patient in that situation begins to rebel and finds ways to slip away from his 'caretaker'. Frequently, that's precisely when a problem develops."

"And tying up a doctor full-time is probably a waste of medical talent."

"That's true, also. I honestly believe that the admiral should have many more years of productive life once we settle this cardiac problem if he can also get his diabetes under control."

"Can you recommend anything along those lines?"

"Of course, I studied the basics in medical school but for this you really need the services of an endocrinologist or Certified Diabetes Educator. Either of them will have spent many years of intense study learning precisely how to deal with diabetes."

"Thank you, Doctor, let's go talk to Kirk."

****

"Where have you been?"

"To make a long story short, I've been lost in the woods."

"Couldn't you simply call for help?"

"Everything we had that was powered by a Montogmery field simply stopped working. That included my legs and our communicators. We spent a long time fighting strange creatures with improvised primitive weapons while trying to find our way back to civilization. When we finally got back, I found you here."

"It sounds as if we've both had a very difficult 'vacation'."

"At least we both survived and this is Doctor du Beers who is prepared to fix what ails you. He wants to explain exactly what he has in mind."

Kirk was stunned when he learned of the extreme damage to his heart. Dr du Beers explained that without the surgery, he would never be able to live disconnected from the Medoo life-support equipment. I hadn't been fully aware of the fact but I learned that the only thing keeping him alive after the heart attack until medical help arrived was my twin sister, Easy, and her phenomenal telekinetic mind. She had mentally 'reached in' to his chest and kept a nearly dead heart operating for several minutes.

Dr. du Beers went on to carefully explain and show his invention.

"Of course, artificial hearts have been around for a long time with varying amounts of success but mine is the first to use a Montgomery field for power and also to move the blood. That minimizes damage to blood tissue. Another unique feature is that the heart senses adrenaline in the blood stream and adjusts output just as a natural heart does. It also measures and adjusts to blood oxygen levels.

"It's really small!"

"Yes, it's less than half the size of the average adult human heart. That's what gave Mr. Montgomery the idea to use two. And after your recent experience with that cloud of mineral dust cutting off your power, Mr. Montogmery also wants back-up power. We should have room for a sixty-day rechargeable power supply that will be kept at full charge by the Montgomery field."

"As much as I tease Scotty, he's not playing games here."

"So, Admiral, Commander, will both of you agree to the surgery?"

"You want me to sign a paper giving a kid permission to cut out my heart?"

"Essentially, yes."

"Well, it's either that or spend a long time lying in this bed doing absolutely nothing. What do you think, Free?"

"We've had a lot of fun in a lot of beds but that one doesn't look so good. Let's get you fixed and back into our bed."

"Where do I sign, Doctor?"

"I don't have the forms with me but I'm sure some paper-pusher will have them. I'll start getting things together and let you know when we're ready. Just don't go anyplace." He smiled.

"What do you think of your doctor?" I asked Kirk after Dr. du Beers left.

"He makes Patrick look old."

I told Kirk what Dr. du Beers had told me about his background."

"I'd feel better if I could talk to someone who actually knows him."

"Scotty's medical foundation has been backing his research since he graduated Harvard. Apparently they think he knows what he's doing."

"But does he know which end of a scalpel to hang onto?"

"He'll be surrounded by experienced Medoo doctors."

"That helps a lot. They're good."

My communicator beeped.

"Commander James, Starship *Leonard Wood* is landing alongside *Enterprise* presently."

"Maybe you should go greet Bones. It's cinch they won't give me a pass."

"Okay; I'll be back later. Maybe he'll want to visit too."

Leonard John McCoy had been one of the earliest trainees aboard the *Enterprise*. He had been top student at Star Fleet Academy and won the chance to train directly under Kirk. He had more than distinguished himself and earned his own starship which he named after his ancestor, Leonard Wood.

But we also learned that John, as he preferred to be called, had been pushed by his physician father and nurse mother to attend medical school. He had obtained his medical degree before entering Star Fleet Academy but had never chosen a specialty. Therefore, he was truly Doctor Leonard McCoy and had served aboard the *Enterprise*. But now he was Captain John McCoy commanding Starship *Leonard Wood*.

"Bones!" Kirk couldn't resist giving John that nickname. I think after a while he had come to like it. I followed the soubriquet with a warm hug.

"I'm happy to see you, Free, but I hear that the Admiral is in bad shape."

"It's serious but the doctors think they can fix it. That part you just brought is part of the system. The whole thing is experimental but Scotty has a lot of faith in Doctor du Beers and I have a lot of faith in Scotty."

"du Beers? ERICH duBeers????"

"I think that is his first name. Do you know him?"

"If it's the same Erich du Beers, he and I were in medical school together and did our cardiology rotations at the same time."

"Does he know what he's doing?"

"He's the real deal. Even in school he had plans for an artificial heart. Is that what he's here to do for the Admiral?"

"Yes, it seems that he perfected his device just as Kirk's heart gave out. Kirk is being kept alive on life support while Dr. du Beers prepares for surgery."

"If I had to bet my life on someone, Erich would be near the top of the list."

"Do me a favor? Go tell that to Kirk. He's scared to death."

****

Kirk was even happy to shake John's hand. Usually Kirk has a strong aversion to handshaking but he made an exception this time.

"You're looking good, John."

"You look better than I expected, Admiral."

"Well, they tell me that some parts of me aren't doing so well."

"Yeah, I talked to your doctors on the way in. That heart has seen better days and your pancreas isn't far behind. The kidneys will need some tender loving care but I think you can keep them going for a long time."

"You expect ME to keep going for a long time?"

"I don't see why not if you let Erich perform the surgery. The other things can be handled."

"You know Doctor du Beers?"

"We studied cardiology together. He went on into research and I dropped out of medicine to pursue a career with Star Fleet. But he's the absolute best."

"So he knows what he's doing?"

"He's a natural at surgery. I observed him a few times and marveled at his dexterity. And from what he's shown me of his system, it would be pretty tough to screw it up anyway. The average thoracic surgeon could do this job in less than an hour."

"I do hope he won't get over-confident."

"I expect that he'll take extra time just making sure that everything is right. Let's face it; his reputation and career are riding on this too."

"And he's backed by the Medoo, who are the finest doctors in the galaxy."

"Not only that, he asked me to be his human assistant."

"YOU???"

"He was top of the class in cardiology, I was a close second."

"And yet you chose to boss a starship."

"Space has been my dream since I was a small boy. My parents chose a career in medicine for me. I know I have a knack for it but my heart is in space."

"Perhaps Star Fleet needs to build a hospital ship and put you in charge of it."

"Now we're beginning to hum the same tune."

"After this mess is over, I'll talk to Scotty."

Doctor du Beers was proceeding with his plans for surgery. The next day, the *Freedom Seven*, commanded by our son, Patrick, arrived bringing not two but three artificial hearts. The factory had fabricated an extra one just in case Dr. du Beers found a problem with one. He

262

immediately set about examining all three units and promised to select the best two.

In the mean time, Kirk and I were enjoying a reunion with Patrick. It hadn't really been so long since we'd seen him; it only felt like forever. His duties with Star Fleet had been keeping him on patrol on the far side of the galaxy and while we had talked often by communicator, there's nothing like person-to-person contact.

"I've seen you looking healthier, Dad."

"I've felt healthier, Son. They tell me I should have been taking better care of myself for a long time and now it's catching up with me."

"You've known for a long time about the diabetes but didn't do anything?"

"My doctor told me about it several years ago and recommended a strict diet along with prescribing pills and suggesting I attend classes for newly diagnosed diabetics. I didn't feel sick so I guess I figured it would go away."

"Well it didn't go away; it almost killed you. Are you ready to listen now?"

"I believe that listening time has arrived."

"Good, because there's someone I want you to meet. Don't go away." He grinned and went to the door where he motioned to someone outside.

In a moment the door was entered by a youngish thirty-something lady. She was fairly tall with curly, medium-length dark brown hair, dark hazel eyes, beautiful high cheek bones and a slim figure. She was far from a beauty queen but I was sure Kirk would be attracted to her. (I was interested myself.)

"Hello, Admiral, Commander. My name is Kimberly Knowlton and I'm a Certified Diabetes Educator as well as a nutritionist.

General Robinson thought that you might be in need of my services but has been unable to contact either of you directly so she had me catch a ride here on the *Freedom Seven*. If you don't want me, I'll hitch the first available ride back to Earth."

"Let's get to know you before we put you on that ship for Earth." Kirk smiled.

"To start, I've read all of your books and I'm not a member of Star Fleet so I shouldn't salute you and I know that you strongly dislike hand shaking but you love kissing. I suppose I should greet you with a kiss."

It wasn't the kind of chaste kiss you'd expect to see given to a man in a sick bed. To me, it looked as if she wanted him to drag her into bed with him. It went on for a very long time.

Then she turned to me.

"Commander James, forgive me. I've been a huge fan of the admiral's for a very long time and I got carried away. From reading his books I know that neither of you has jealousy trouble so I 'went for it.' I hope you don't mind."

"I don't own him and I've watched him kiss a lot of other women. Just as he's watched me kiss many other men... and women."

"I take your hint. I was planning to kiss you right after I kissed the admiral but I chickened out. You see, I've never actually kissed a woman although it's always been a fantasy of mine and the admiral's books really got me thinking about it."

"You want to kiss me?"

"Well, yeah, but I don't know how to start."

"Do you want me to kiss you?"

"Oh, would you?"

So I slowly and gently took her in my arms and pressed my lips to hers. I kept my mouth shut, giving her a chance to get used to the idea,

She was stiff at first but after a few seconds her lips softened then her tongue probed my lips, seeking entrance. I allowed it and then she was exploring my mouth fully. Soon, one of her hands was behind my head, pulling me closer while the other hand was fondling a breast and tweaking the nipple.

After a long while, we came up for air.

"I like this." She panted.

"I do too."

"Can we do more?"

"Well, here and now wouldn't be good but perhaps we can table the matter."

"I want you to teach me everything."

"I'll be glad to."

"As soon as I calm down, I should get back to the real reason I'm here."

Patrick took his cue and fetched us some iced tea. After a short 'social break', she was capable of business as usual.

"Well, after what just happened, I suppose both of you should call me 'Kim' and I hope I may call you 'Free' and 'Kirk'."

We agreed to that.

"To start over, I'm Irene Robinson's daughter. I had a brief and disastrous marriage that left me with the name Knowlton. As I stated, I'm a Certified Diabetes Educator as well as a nutritionist. I was associated with an endocrinologist and working through his office until he lost his license to practice medicine; he got caught fooling around with his female patients. I just don't earn enough to support my own office. I was looking to join another practice when Mother suggested I come to work

265

for Star Fleet as a civilian consultant and to help you. I've been a big fan of your books since the first was published so I jumped at the chance and here I am. I do hope you'll let me stay."

"And exactly what can you do for us?"

"I can teach you how to deal with your diabetes. I spoke with your Medoo doctors and there's no doubt now that you've progressed to type one diabetes. That means that your pancreas is essentially useless. I know that sounds scary but it also means that we can use a device I brought along just in case."

"A device?"

"Yes. For many, many years medical science has been working towards the 'artificial pancreas'. Unfortunately, they don't have one yet but I brought the newest advancement in the evolution. A researcher recently obtained approval for an implantable glucose monitor. This monitor can give real-time accurate readings of your blood sugar and send them to an insulin pump. The pump will then automatically infuse the correct amount of insulin to maintain a proper blood sugar. One big drawback of the monitor is that the sensor must be placed deeply within a major blood vessel such as the aorta. Another downside is the possibility of low blood sugars. When that happens, you need to be able to recognize the symptoms and correct them quickly."

"Insulin pump?"

"It will be a big step; going from essentially no treatment directly to a pump but that's what I'm here for. Usually a diabetic spends years treating with diet and pills then starts injecting insulin. If the diabetes gets bad enough, a pump is considered."

"So you're suggesting that this sensor be implanted along with the artificial heart."

266

"Yes. There'll be a small implanted control box also but it doesn't take up much room. It's powered by a Montgomery field and has a ninety-day battery backup in case of field failure. The external pump will need to be maintained often and I can teach you to do that."

"Maintained?"

"The insulin reservoir inside it will need to be refilled about every three days and the cannula, or injection site, will need to be moved. The procedure is nearly painless and most people say it's less uncomfortable than injecting insulin."

"So what's the bottom line?"

"Even with the sensor and the pump, you'll still have diabetes. That means you'll need to watch your diet; no going hog-wild at dessert bars. But within reason, you can eat almost anything you want. The sensor will determine the amount of glucose in your blood and administer the correct dosage of insulin to cover it."

"It sounds as if we're going to need you."

"I'm not the only person who knows about these things but I hope you want to keep me around."

Kirk caught my eye and I gave him a little nod.

"I believe that we've decided we want you. Call your mother and tell her to put you on the payroll full time. As soon as we get back to the *Enterprise*, we'll figure out living arrangements for you."

"Kirk, for the time being, why not let her share our bed? You'll be here for a while and I get lonely."

"The bed's big enough for all three of us if that suits her once I get out of here."

267

"Let's see what the doctors have to say about that first."

In keeping with Kirk's policy of not writing porn, I won't go into detail about that night. Kim was sweet and eager to learn; we had a good time and neither of us got much sleep.

The next day, we visited Kirk together.

"From the expressions of both of your faces, I'd say you had fun."

"It would have been more fun with you there."

"I doubt these wires and tubes would stretch that far."

"And even that high-tech Medoo life support equipment might have trouble keeping up with the activity."

"So let's hope they get the show on the road here."

"That's exactly what I have in mind." Dr. du Beers spoke as he came in the door. "The *Sacajawea* has just arrived from Arisia bringing the specially designed control computer, Once I have time to assemble and test the entire system, we can proceed with the surgery."

"Why did the computer take so long?" Kirk asked.

"The Arisians designed a molecular computer to my specifications and then 'grew' it. The essential programming is 'hard-wired' into its circuitry so no outside agency can possibly affect it. Other functions can be 'fine tuned' externally. The entire complex computer is no larger than a pin head but the wiring interface is considerably larger in order to facilitate connection into the system."

"Will you be able to accommodate the glucose sensor?" Kim wanted to know.

"I spoke with Doctor Kannen, who invented and developed that system. We decided together that the sensor will go into the output 'Y' where the two artificial hearts are connected to the aorta. She feels it will be the ideal location and it will be very convenient to install during the surgery. I can mount the sensor hardware directly to the cardiac package."

"Isn't this 'package' getting awfully large?" Kirk was beginning to fret.

"Actually, the two hearts, the computer, the glucose sensor with its hardware, and the backup batteries all together make up a package slightly smaller than the average human heart. And over the years, your heart disease has caused your heart to enlarge so we're going to have some excess room."

"Could you put that insulin pump in there too?"

"It would be a tight fit and then you'd find it very inconvenient opening your chest every three days to refill the reservoir. Insulin doesn't keep very long if it isn't refrigerated so you can't have a larger reservoir."

"So I'm stuck taking insulin for the rest of my life?"

"Probably, unless someone finds a definitive cure for diabetes. There are many researchers working on precisely that and several seem to be making progress. I certainly hope someone has a breakthrough soon."

"You sound as if it's personal."

"I was diagnosed with type one diabetes at the age of six. I gave myself injections for many years and now wear an insulin pump. I hope to soon be a candidate for the system I'm installing in you."

"Even though it requires major surgery?"

"After almost thirty years of poking holes in my fingers several times a day, I'll do almost anything."

"I know what you mean. The constant testing was the main reason I didn't properly take care of my diabetes; it was just too much trouble."

"And if you move around a lot you need to take the meter with you then remember to stop and test. I know exactly what you mean; it's much easier to just ignore the diabetes. However, that's the way a lot of people get into trouble."

"You can bet I'll be paying attention from now on; I can't afford to lose any more vital organs."

"Absolutely correct. Your heart is done for but I'm about to replace that. Your pancreas is essentially useless but the sensor and insulin pump will fill in for that. Your kidneys are in bad shape and will need a lot of care. Kim will help you with a diet that can help them. Your doctor can also give you medication to help. I know she has you taking an anti-cholesterol medication and you'll need to keep on top of that. The last thing you need now is a pulmonary embolism or a stroke. All of these dangers are exacerbated by diabetes. Once you get it under control, the danger lessens considerably."

"That settles it. Kim is definitely moving in with us."

"Moving in is more than most diabetics do but working closely with a Certified Diabetes Educator is a very wise decision. And a nutritionist is another great ally. And in this case, she's both. Let her guide you because she knows exactly what she's talking about."

"So you approve?"

270

"It's not up to me to approve or disapprove of your personal lifestyle. I've read your books and I ENVY your lifestyle but I won't comment further. I can say for certain that your heart will be able to handle the strain with no difficulty. The rest of your body.... well, that's for other doctors to say. From what I know of diabetes, having a nutritionist and CDE close by will be an enormous help in learning how to deal with it. But it's important for you to know these things too, for the times when you're on your own. Don't count on others to always do your thinking for you."

"It appears that things are finally coming together."

"Speaking of things coming together, I left Scotty checking out that Arisian computer, Once he's satisfied that it'll do exactly what we want it to do, I'll begin assembling the package for implantation. All the other sub-assemblies have been inspected and approved. After assembly, we'll schedule surgery, possibly tomorrow or the next day."

"You're not taking any chances with this, are you?"

"You're not only my first and most important patient; my entire reputation is riding on this surgery. If anything goes wrong, twenty years of my hopes and dreams are out the window."

"Please try not to get overly nervous."

"Getting nervous messes with my blood sugar; I'll just have to control it." He grinned. I'll keep you up to date and let you know when we schedule the procedure."

After he left, the three of us chatted aimlessly for a while then somehow we got onto the subject of kissing. I insisted that Kirk was a better kisser than I was but Kim wasn't so sure.

271

"I only got to kiss her once and she caught me by surprise." He protested.

"When he gets out of here with a fully-operational heart, he'll show you what kissing is all about." I assured her.

"There's no time like the present." Kirk countered. I think he was bored. (And horny.)

So Kim moved to his bedside for a 'demonstration'.

It looked as if Kirk really got into this one. He was in a semi-sitting position in the hospital bed and he managed to pull her into his lap before getting her into one of his patented liplocks. From watching the chin movements, I could tell there was plenty of tongue action and his hands were well-involved. I don't know about them, but I was breathing hard and starting to sweat from just watching.

For those of you who haven't read Kirk's journals, the Medoo are dedicated medical professionals who are from a planet on the far side of the galaxy from Earth. They spend much of their time cruising the stars attempting to dispense medical aid to anyone . who needs it.

The Medoo, however, are a strange-looking race. Their physical appearance is much like an Earthly garden slug although much larger. The average adult Medoo is about eight feet from the tip of the 'snout' to the tip of the tail but the forward half is normally carried in an upright posture so the Medoo will 'stand' about four feet tall. They have two manipulating appendages which are very similar to octopus arms minus the suction cups and the arms 'branch out' near the ends into fine 'fingers'.

The Medoo have no features on their heads other than two eyes on short stalks. Hearing and speaking are accomplished by a round diaphragm located on what would be the throat of most creatures and breathing is accomplished through a series of small spiracles along both sides of the 'neck'. Eating is done through a mouth located in the single 'foot', which is on the lower side of the body.

The Medoo come from a very wet planet and therefore must keep their bodies moist at all times. In our environment, they wear a fabric covering across the back along with a bag or pouch or water with a small pump that keeps the fabric and their bodies moist.

So during this 'demonstration', a Medoo 'nurse' hurried into the room at a full gallop for a Medoo, which would be a quick walk for a human, to see what was going on.

It seemed that Kirk's vital signs, which had been stable, were now acting very strangely. His oxygen intake and sugar requirements were off the scale and the nurse was very concerned.

This, of course, ended our 'kissing contest'. We decided to talk about safer subjects and reserve sex for more appropriate venues.

Next topic: cooking. Kim, like Kirk turned out to be a gourmet chef so I decided right there to hang up my frying pan. Kirk was describing some of his favorite recipes and Kim was making suggestions for making them more diabetic-friendly. Many of them actually sounded better Kim's way.

I decided that we wouldn't starve. Of course, I've always loved salads and could easily become a vegetarian. Kirk, however, dislikes most vegetables and could starve to death at the world's largest salad bar. Kim took that in stride and made suggestions that seemed to suit Kirk.

"Remember, Kirk, your kidney problem means other dietary restrictions. Along with

273

medication, we'll need to reduce your protein intake in order to take some of the load off your kidneys. That means smaller portions of meats and cheese but we can make up for it with larger portions of other things you like."

"How do you plan to do that?"

"Just as an example: one of your favorite recipes is Chinese pepper steak. You simply use about half as much meat and increase the peppers and onions. That way, you get the same flavors and almost exactly the same nutrition with considerably less protein along with less fat. You can also use a reduced sodium soy sauce in the roux for the gravy. That shouldn't significantly affect the taste but the results will be much healthier for you."

"I guess we can give that a try."

"We can 'tweek' most of the recipes you like in order to make them better for you. And I have tons of other recipes you might enjoy. There's only one way to find out."

"The proof is in the pudding."

"I have some great pudding recipes, too."

"Now all I have to do is survive having my heart removed."

"Strike 'removed' and put in 'replaced'. We all need to have confidence in Doctor du Beers." She would make a great cheerleader.

The next day, Kim and I were visiting Kirk bright and early despite the fact that we had been up fairly late.

About mid-morning, Dr. du Beers and Scotty breezed in and the good doctor was carrying a box about the size of an old-fashioned shoe box while Scotty had a large manila envelope.

"We hope you'll consider this to be good news: Scotty and I both checked out the various components and could find absolutely no problems. Therefore, we burned the midnight oil assembling the implant and the unit is ready for implantation. Is the recipient ready?"

"Just exactly what is this thing like?" Kirk was a little apprehensive.

"I figured you would have questions so we brought the actual unit along with photographs of the assembly process." Erich was well-prepared.

He reached into the box and removed an item.

"This is a standard plastic model of an average healthy human heart. I brought it along for comparison. And this is the unit we intend to implant.

He displayed something that looked remarkably like a heart but less complicated.

"After assembly, we encased the entire unit in a non-reactive sheath to protect both the components and the delicate tissues of your body. Just prior to implantation, it will be thoroughly sterilized."

"It looks terribly small."

"It actually has the ability to move more than twice the amount of blood than the natural heart but your body couldn't handle that volume.

275

The Arisian computer is programmed to keep the output down to a manageable level at all times while maintaining the proper supply to the body. This unit, in contrast to previous artificial hearts, can sense blood oxygen levels and adrenaline levels and adjust blood flow in accordance with those demands. It does not, however, have the nerve connections of the natural heart so it won't function in exactly the same manner."

"Which means?"

"In times of stress such as fright or anger, your adrenaline levels will naturally increase. With a natural heart, your pulse would increase to match. With this unit, you have no pulse but the heart will increase output until the adrenaline level drops and then reduce blood flow to a more normal level."

"How will that be different?"

"For one thing, have you ever experienced the 'shakes' after a 'fight-o-flight' situation?"

"Many, many times."

"That shouldn't happen with this unit because the heart output is more closely tied to the adrenaline level. As you calm down emotionally, your heart 'catches up'."

"So this heart is superior to a natural one?"

276

"Well, I wouldn't recommend replacing a healthy heart with one of these but you certainly won't be losing by this surgery. Once the surgical incision heals, you should feel better and stronger than you have in many years. And I understand that the Medoo have some very advanced closure procedures that I'm eager to learn."

"They performed major surgery on some of our battle wounded and they were back on duty in surprisingly short times."

"Can you give me an example?"

"I had a gunner with a serious abdominal wound. The Medoo were forced to perform a bowel resection and the gunner was back on duty two days later. When I offered him more time to recuperate, he told me that there was no need; he was in no pain and everything was operating perfectly."

"That is impressive. Even with a Montgomery field to clean the wound, a wounded bowel can be a very messy surgery. And traditionally, a long recovery."

He and Scotty went on to show us the third artificial heart, the one they decided not to use in the assembly and they showed us photographs of assembly of the final unit.

I noticed something and just had to ask.

"It looks as if there are more pieces than the original drawing. Did you add more?"

"You have a good eye for detail. Because we had the room, Scotty added more rechargeable batteries so now the unit will have about ninety days of independence from outside power. If Kirk ever finds himself in a situation such as you did recently, his heart will keep operating for up to three months. And as soon as he returns to a normal power situation, the batteries recharge."

"And I believe you said that the essential functions are 'hard wired' so they can't be affected by outside influences."

"That's quite correct. The system can be slightly adjusted by a coded signal from a control unit but the basic functions cannot be affected by strong magnetic or any other influences."

"If he won't have a pulse, how will we keep track of his medical well-being?"

"The unit has sensors built in and will send telemetry to medical monitoring units. He'll be given a special wristwatch so he can keep track of the most important data and his doctors will have equipment for more detailed examinations."

"It sounds like you have the bases covered."

"I certainly hope so; I've spent a lot of years thinking about this and working on it. Now I have the awesome Scott Montgomery backing me up."

"He's a good man to have in your corner."

"And Montgomery Medical Manufacturing is a great place for building prototypes."

"I only had to offer some huge bonuses for two perfect models of Erich's units, fast. The factory turned out three and let us choose. All three passed every test we could devise with flying colors so I guess I'll have to write some checks."

"You know all you have to do is tell a lawyer and the checks get written."

"That's true; I rarely even get to sign my own name."

"Back to my original question: is the recipient ready?" Erich interjected.

Kirk sought my eyes and held them with a questioning look. I gave him a half-scared / half-confident mini-nod.

He cleared his throat. "Well, Doctor. Since my only other choice is to spend the remainder of my life, such as it is, wired to this bed, and I've come to believe in you and your device: sharpen your knife."

279

"I'm sure the Medoo will have an operating theatre ready but let me go make arrangements. I also need to alert Doctor McCoy to make sure he plans to be sober tomorrow morning." He grinned. (In all the time since I met John, I've never seen nor heard of him taking a drink of alcohol.)

"And I should call Dick to let him know what we decided." Dick is Kirk's brother who runs a horse and pony ranch in Wyoming back on Earth.

While Kirk was talking to Dick, I took Kim and Scotty aside and introduced them as they hadn't met until now. They soon warmed to each other and before long they were 'kissing friends' and discussing further action. For a lady who had only read about the swinging lifestyle, Kim was catching on quickly.

Scotty promised to bring Easy to the 'Admiral's Suite' tonight to meet Kim; none of us expected to get much sleep anyway and since we were going to be awake, we might as well be awake together. Kirk would naturally be sedated before surgery in order to ensure a good night's sleep. Easy would have been there with us visiting Kirk but she regularly volunteered in the *Enterprise* sick bay and this was her scheduled shift.

The three of us remained with Kirk until the nurse came to administer his sedation. He (she? it?) assured us that he would rest comfortably until shortly before time for

280

surgery. After that, we stopped by Scotty's cabin to collect Easy then went to dinner in the *Enterprise* dining facility then retired to the Admiral's Suite.

Kirk and I have the biggest bed I have ever seen. When we need new sheets (often), we need to have them custom-made on Earth and shipped to us because no standard bed even approaches ours in size. It has gravity control so we can become nearly weightless when we want with a light force field at the sides to prevent 'drifting out' at the sides into higher gravity. The headboard contains a complex communications console so Kirk or I can be reached in an emergency and it even has beverage dispensers. Scotty custom designed the bed and even the entire suite for us when Kirk accepted the job as Fleet Admiral to the Federation Galactic Fleet.

So after beginning slowly, the bed was soon piled with naked bodies. Again, I'm not going into details because you can find porn almost anywhere in books, movies, or the web. But trust me, if you can find it in porn, it probably happened in that bed that night.

After a long while, Scotty was on his back in the center of the bed receiving attention from all three of us adoring women when he suddenly didn't look good at all. He curled into a fetal position and was obviously in pain.

"Scotty? What's wrong?"

Easy quickly got 'that look' on her face and I knew she was using the wonderful mental powers she had 'downloaded' from the Arachna.

"Now HE'S having a heart attack! Call sick bay and I'll try to keep his heart going."

"Sick Bay, Medical emergency in the Admiral's Suite! Suspected heart attack! Need full medical response! Stat!" Communications is my profession and they taught in an emergency to give only the important facts.

So once again, Easy used her marvelous telekinetic powers to keep a heart operating while she waited anxiously for medical assistance.

It really wasn't long; it only felt like a couple centuries before the emergency medical team burst through the door.

They were professionals; they wasted little time ogling three nude ladies and set directly to work on Scotty.

Easy briefly stopped her 'mental CPR' so they could get an honest assessment.

"No pulse!"

"I'll resume CPR until you're ready."

"OK"

The tech quickly began attaching EKG leads.

Once the EKG was attached, they had a picture of the situation.

"V-Fib!"

They found it necessary to defibrillate him three times before he was stable enough to suit them. After that, they administered IVs and transferred him to a gurney for transport to Sick Bay.

As they left, I pulled on a pair of legs and started dressing. Easy and Kim were dressing too.

"Could you tell how bad it is, Easy?"

"I'm afraid it's almost as bad as Kirk. He hasn't had a checkup in the time I've known him and who knows how long before that? He lives on cereal and coffee, eats whenever and whatever, and doesn't get enough sleep then he works himself to death. I should have seen this coming."

"At least you were here to keep him alive."

"It was so bad, I doubt that conventional CPR would have done much good."

"Shouldn't he have been having some kind of warning symptoms before now?"

"I'm no medical professional but I would think so. I hope we get a chance to ask him about it."

We hurried to Sick Bay where we found Scotty slightly improved but still unconscious.

We found Doctor Lee Chen attending Scotty.

"Doctor, can you tell us how he is?"

He took us to a consulting room where he laid it all out:

"Commander Montgomery has suffered a severe myocardial infarction. A large portion of the heart muscle is involved and it appears that any recovery will be minimal. As you know, we don't have a cardiologist aboard this ship and given the availability of the Medoo hospital ship, my recommendation is that he be transferred there as quickly as possible; they have much better training and facilities for dealing with this kind of difficulty."

Easy told him what she had said to us.

"As I mentioned, I'm no cardiologist but bad food, little sleep, and overwork are generally conducive to heart trouble. Commander Montgomery's excesses are legendary and this frankly doesn't surprise me. However, he is such a wonderful man that he's worth any amount of effort to save. Therefore, we'll do everything we can."

"So how do you propose to handle things?"

"We are keeping him stable while watching him carefully. I've contacted the Medoo hospital ship and they're sending a life-support shuttle to transport him back to their ship. Once there, well, they have yet to lose a patient under their care."

Easy smiled through her frightened tears. "Thank you, Doctor, you did all I could ask."

So the three of us made the short trek back to the Medoo ship, *Mother of Mercy*.

Scotty had been ensconced in the room adjacent to Kirk's so we didn't need to be wandering far in the hallways. The Medoo don't have arbitrary 'visiting hours' but if the nurse thinks your visit is bad for the patient, you're out the door and arguments do you no good. As long as the patient benefits, you can stay 24/7. Food and even visitor's beds will be provided.

Doctor Perla is not only the captain of the *Mother of Mercy*, he's a fine doctor of medicine. We were fortunate to find him attending Scotty when we arrived.

"So we have a second human cardiac patient."

"Yes, Doctor, and although they aren't truly related, they grew up as brothers and have been very close all their lives."

"Of course, we do everything in our power to preserve the lives of all our patients but that makes them very special. Commander Montgomery has suffered very severe damage to the heart muscle and I seriously doubt that we can repair it. In cases such as this, we often recommend a replacement."

"Have you spoken with Doctor du Beers?"

Doctor du Beers is scheduled for surgery early in the morning and I hesitate to disturb him so late at night. The Doctor's alertness may be the difference for Admiral James."

"Can you keep Commander Montgomery alive indefinitely?"

"Oh, certainly. With our life support, he can remain alive even without a functioning heart. However, he probably will not regain consciousness until his cardiac function improves."

"Keep him alive at all costs. I have an idea."

After the doctor left, Easy and Kim drowned me in questions.

The questions essentially boiled down to one: What are you thinking?

"Erich and Scotty both said that only one of those heart units is really necessary but they're using two in Kirk just being over-cautious. The same goes for the switching computer and battery backup. They have another perfectly good artificial heart; why not use it for Scotty?"

We didn't even bother asking for visitor's beds. Most of the remaining night was passed in pacing the floors and walking between rooms, checking on both our 'main men'. My prosthetic legs are powered and never become fatigued but the upper thighs above them are flesh and bone so they do get tired. I'm sure Kim and Easy were both near exhaustion when Doctor du Beers appeared.

"The nurses tell me that we now have another patient."

"Yes, Doctor. Scotty dropped in his tracks last night."

"I took a quick glance at his chart and it doesn't look good."

"That's what Doctor Perla told us. We know you're getting ready to operate on Kirk but are you up for another surgery soon?"

"What do you have in mind?"

"You said that only one unit is really necessary and you have one unit left. Can you use that unit to save Scotty?"

"You caught me off-guard with that one. Let me think a moment." He paused and pondered.

"I think I have a better idea. If everyone agrees, how about two simultaneous surgeries?"

"Can you hold a scalpel in each hand?"

"Certainly not. What I have in mind is for me to proceed with the operation on Admiral James assisted by a human thoracic surgeon while John, Dr. McCoy, performs the procedure on Commander Montgomery assisted by another thoracic surgeon. All of the Medoo operating suites have dual tables so we can work in the same room and talk to each other as we work."

"Is Dr. McCoy qualified for this?"

"I tried to convince him back in school that he should go into cardiology. He's a natural at it and many times, he knew more than the professors."

"But will he do it?"

"We can only ask him. But the sooner Scotty has surgery, the better his chances."

■■■■■■■■■■■■■■■■■■■■■■■■■■■■■■■■■■■■

"ME?!?! Operate???? I don't even have a license to practice medicine."

"If you want to be picky, I don't either. But we're a long way from Earth and the two of us are by far the most qualified cardiologists available. I've located two very good thoracic

288

surgeons to back us up but neither knows a lot about hearts. Both patients deserve the best we can give them and that's us."

"But I've never even attempted anything so complex and never without supervision."

"Neither of us has but this specific surgery has never been attempted before by anyone. Consider it to be ground-breaking surgery. We'll supervise each other."

So when the dust settled, John would be assisted by Dr. Steven Readinger, an eminent thoracic surgeon from the *Enterprise* while Erich drew Dr. Pavel Patel of the *Leonard Wood*. Filling in the surgical team would be an experienced crew of Medoo nurses and doctors.

"As frightening as this procedure may seem, it really is less complicated than a surgery such as a quadruple bypass. However, we expect to take plenty of time, making sure we get everything right the first time. The Medoo life support equipment allows us the luxury of time so we expect to take full advantage of it." Erich explained.

We watched the support staff take the men we love off to surgery with mixed emotions of hope, confidence, and apprehension. Had we made the right decision? Would both of them survive? No matter how long the surgery took, it would be too long.

The Medoo measure time differently from us but my wristwatch told me that they had begun surgery at about eight o:clock AM. When my watch told me that noon was approaching, I asked the nurse in charge of the area for lunch trays for the three of us. They brought us something but don't ask me what it was. It must have tasted fairly good because all three of us ate well but our minds were elsewhere.

Finally, at about three PM by my watch, a nurse came and asked us to clear the room for a few minutes.

"Why is that?"

"We need to re-arrange the furniture. We will be placing both patients in this room when they return."

"Will they be returning soon?"

"They are on the way now."

Kirk was brought in first followed closely by Scotty. The Medoo hospital beds were used as transport also so there was no need to shift them from gurney to bed. Surprisingly, there was no life support equipment connected, not even oxygen, to either patient. Both, however, were asleep.

"They should be waking soon. The doctors will be in as soon as they change clothing." The nurse left us to admire our men.

True to the nurse's word Erich and John were there in only a few moments. Frankly, they both looked worse than Kirk or Scotty. The two of them appeared to need a good meal followed by about a week's sleep.

"Well, I'd say they came through the procedures better than we did. Of course, all they needed to do was sleep." Erich quipped.

"Everyone, Kirk is waking!" Kim called.

We crowded around Kirk's bed and he opened his eyes. The first place he looked was into my eyes.

"I love you, Honey. Is it over?"

"Yes, Hon, it's over and you came through it fine. Erich did a great job and now you have a heart that will outlive you."

"I feel stronger already. In fact, other than a slight ache in my chest, I feel better than I have in years."

"The Medoo have some awesome surgical closure techniques. A little gadget causes instant healing of the bone and incision as soon as it's applied. I didn't need wires or sutures and you're healed completely now. In fact, as soon as you feel up to it, you can be discharged from the hospital."

"Perhaps I should rest just a little."

"And we want to see about Scotty."

"Scotty?"

So we told him what had happened to Scotty then stood back so he could see his almost-brother lying in the other bed.

"Is he okay?"

"He should be waking soon."

"He's waking now!" Easy called.

Kim, Easy, and I crowded around Scotty so we would be the first persons he saw.

He opened his eyes.

"Ladies, that was the most intense orgasm I ever experienced. But how did the three of you get dressed so quickly? And where are we?"

So we had quite a lot of explaining to do to Scotty. His memory stopped with the four of us having fun together in bed. He'd been unconscious since and had no memory of the preparations for surgery.

"Wow! Do you have any idea what would have happened if I hadn't survived?"

"We would have been very upset......"

"But think of Earth's economy. My lawyers would have all needed heart implants

292

next. It really could have caused a major catastrophe."

"I never even thought of that. To us, you're simply the man we love."

"Well, it's over now and I seem to be still alive. I suppose I'll have to tell the lawyers about it but actually now my potential life span is increased so it's all for the better. Thank you, Erich."

"It was John, Doctor McCoy, who performed your surgery."

"Bones?!? I didn't know you had it in you!"

"To tell the truth, I didn't either. But I studied cardiology and Erich was busy with Kirk so I figured somebody should take care of you."

"I feel really good. Much stronger than I have in a long time."

It wasn't long before the two of them were walking around the room and even doing simple calisthenics. Doctor Perla dropped by to consult with Eric and John and the three decided that if Kirk and Scotty tolerated dinner well enough they could be discharged.

"Kirk, you'll be getting a diabetic-friendly meal. It'll also be low protein and reduced sodium because you need to get used to the new order of things. Scotty, you're not diabetic but you need to modify your eating habits too so you'll be getting a special diet too." Kim gave them the bad news.

"I can't just have a couple boxes of dry cereal and a lot of coffee?" Scotty pouted.

"I'm afraid those days are over, Scotty. You need to modify your eating, sleeping, and work habits before another body system shoots craps on you." Kim wasn't pulling any punches.

"Easy, are you going to let her do this to me?"

"Not only LET her, I'm going to back her every step of the way. I want to keep you alive forever."

"Well, it IS my intention to be around for a long time and this little episode just taught me that I'm not indestructible so I suppose this old dog better start learning some new tricks."

"Right. The next thing could be a stroke or kidney failure and there are no quick fixes for those."

"Very high on your 'to do' list should be a visit to Doctor Lee. He's an excellent internist and I'm sure he'll want to start you on some cholesterol-lowering medication. In the mean time, I'll work with you on foods that can help you without you feeling food-deprived." Kim was making herself useful.

"So we all ate a hearty meal and nobody got sick. I guess that means we can leave. What shall we do now?" I recognized 'that look' on my husband's face.

"And should you not remain in your hospital room at least long enough to receive visitors?" Came from the door.

We all turned to the door and saw Mentor and Maitresse entering.

"What are you doing here?" Kirk blurted, perhaps not the most elegant greeting, but heartfelt.

"We managed to 'hitch a ride', as it were, in order to visit our beloved adopted son. And on the way, we learned that another dear one was also in dire straits. We are gratified to find both of you looking so well."

Maitresse had to kiss everyone in the room while Mentor restricted himself to kissing the women. For entities each several hundred thousand years old, they're outstanding kissers.

"Back to a question I asked a while ago: what do we do now:" Kirk persisted.

"What do you want to do?" I asked him.

"This has become a euphemism for a funeral but I want to celebrate life."

"By that, you mean exactly the same thing that put the two of you in here, right?"

"But this time I want to invite the two best cardiologists I know to be there, just in case."

I did a quick calculation. "That's a wise precaution but that would mean one more man than we have women."

"Why not invite Brooke? She's young and cute and she's always up for a party."

I'm not even going to try to describe the debaucheries that night. It seems that, while not a virgin, Erich's experience with the opposite sex was sadly lacking. All of us did our very best to correct it. It's a wonder he didn't need a cardiologist himself before morning.

Scotty and Kirk were still going strongly when most of us were beginning to fade.

"I guess we got more sleep than everyone else."

Kirk eventually called Mentor aside for a conference but asked me to attend.

"Father, are you allowed to be absent from your planet for extended periods?"

"The planet does not own us, My Son. We may come and go as we choose."

"If I decide to tour the galaxy to campaign for emperor, could you come along?"

By now, everyone in the room was listening.

"But, Son, you have always firmly denied any interest in such an occupation."

"I suppose you can say that I've had a change of heart. Perhaps I'm too old to be out troubleshooting. Maybe it's time to sit on a throne and tell others how to do it."

"That all remains to be seen. But yes, I will 'hit the campaign trail' with you."
▪▪▪▪▪▪▪▪▪▪▪▪▪▪▪▪▪▪▪▪▪▪▪▪▪▪▪▪▪▪▪▪▪▪▪

So now I'm going to wrap this up. Kirk is back to being Kirk and I'm sure you can look forward to another of his journals soon. No matter what happens, it's bound to be interesting.

Freedom Marie Johnson James

AFTERWORD
(Well, perhaps several words)

This marks the fifth book I have produced since being bitten by the 'writing bug' in 2007. In the beginning, I knew absolutely nothing about the business of writing, editing, or publishing. I merely wrote a book and just assumed that a publisher would purchase my manuscript and turn me into an instant millionaire. WRONG! Several months and many rejection letters later, it finally sank into my thick head that it just wasn't done that way.

By that time, I had completed the second volume, More Star Tricks, and was beginning to write the third volume.

But what was I to do with all my accumulated work?

One 'generous' fly-by-night publisher offered to put my first book in print if I would pay them $2,500.00 plus finance any advertising. Of course, if I wanted my books in book stores, I would need to purchase the books then convince the stores to stock them. Gee, thanks.

Eventually I discovered Create Space. This publisher accepted my manuscript and will print the books only when ordered. But the books are listed on Amazon.com at a reasonable price and Shazaam! I'm a published author.

Of course, this meant that I must do my own editing and be responsible for the publishing.

I published the first two volumes almost simultaneously and frankly, there were many errors. In looking back over them, I see that I hadn't even learned to keep the paragraph indentations and right margins even.

But I'm learning.

I think you'll see considerable improvement by book three and even more improvement in book four.

This volume, number five, represents a major format change from the 8 X 10" size to 6 X 9".

Frankly, book sales have been sluggish and I suspect that partially to blame could be the unwieldy proportions of the earlier volumes.

But I'm dedicated to delivering an interesting story to you, Dear Reader. So feel free to contact me with comments, questions, and suggestions. I sit up punishing this keyboard until 6:00 AM every morning just so you'll have something to read; let me know what you like.

My email is elrond1951@gmail.com and my snail mail is:

David A. Shaffer

%Shaffer Publishing

4397 W. Bethany Home Road #1146

Glendale, Az. 85301

ABOUT THE AUTHOR

David A. Shaffer was born in Ottumwa, Iowa in the early 50's, or so he's told. He wasn't able to read clock or calendar at the time so he was forced to accept the word of others. A younger brother and sister joined him later and turned out relatively normal despite his best efforts.

David grew up, more or less, in a middle class home in a nice neighborhood.

He attended public schools and graduated high school in 1969 despite his own best efforts to the contrary.

Unfortunately for him, he had tested in the high IQ range and more was expected of him than he cared to do. All he wanted out of school was..... out of school.

Once achieving that goal, he had no idea what to do next. Never a great planner, he hadn't considered this. His mother's family had a tradition of working at a local slaughterhouse so he applied there and was hired. That job only lasted about three years until the plant closed in 1972.

While working at the plant, he had been studying the Chinese martial arts along with flying search and rescue for the Civil Air Patrol. After he lost his job, his sifu (martial arts instructor) asked him to assist in instructing a Defensive Tactics course for the local Police Academy. This led to an interest in law enforcement.

David was able to enroll in the Academy through the local community college. After graduation, he was hired by a small town not far from his hometown as a police dispatcher and shortly thereafter was elevated to part-time patrol / part-time dispatch.

This job continued for a few years but again fate intervened. The city police and sheriff's departments combined their dispatch, eliminating his job.

Fortunately for him, another small town nearby had just lost their night police officer. David applied and was hired. This was a very small town with a population of about two thousand. It was actually a more challenging job because only one officer was on duty at a time and things could become pretty rough.

David remained on this job for several years. During this time he married twice, divorcing once.

304

By 1979, he was becoming dissatisfied with police work and beginning to wish he had applied himself better in school so he could go into medicine, his true interest. After many long discussions with his wife, he took a leave of absence from his job and enlisted in the U. S. Army as a Combat Medic. The Army taught him a lot about medicine but to his dismay, he received no certificates that could be used in civilian life.

Disillusioned with the Army and finding his marriage in trouble at home, he managed to get out of the Army early in 1981. He was rehired by the same small town but this time on the Street Department. He was unable to save his marriage and it ended in divorce. He remained single for many years. During this time, he learned to play electric bass guitar and played in several local country/western bands.

New Year's Eve 1990/91, he met the woman who was to be his third wife. His band was playing in his hometown and he met her there. A brief courtship followed and he married her. This was, as usual, a disaster. The marriage finally ended formally in 1993 but they had been separated much longer than that.

In early 1994, at the request of his first ex-wife, he began dating a woman he didn't really like. Just as a favor. He was trying to 'let the woman down easy' when he suddenly found himself in the hospital. He had suffered a stroke. The woman he had been dating was there caring for him and doing all the things the nurses should have been doing but weren't. When he went home, she went with him and moved in. She stayed nine years.

He was only off work for a short time. Sick pay was limited and he had used his vacation time. But he was never as effective as before. The other employees were 'carrying him' and he didn't like that. He suffered through the indignity for some time while looking into options.

He finally accepted a voluntary layoff in the spring of 1996. He filed for Social Security Disability and the State of Iowa also pays a disability pension.

His personal life began looking up too. He was contacted by a woman he had loved for nearly thirty years but she had been married to a friend of his. Her husband had passed away and she had remarried but was now divorced. She had secretly loved him for all that time too. At about the same time, he discovered that the woman who had been living with him had seriously messed up his finances, putting him on the road to bankruptcy. He threw the other woman out of his house and his true love moved in.

They were happy, at least for a while.

In the spring of 2004, David suffered a heart attack. When he lost his job, he also lost his health insurance so he was treated by the VA. They were unable to do a bypass due to the location of the affected arteries and a heart transplant is not possible because of his diabetes. He was implanted with a defibrillator in case he has another attack and told to forget about working.

Finding the Midwest winters increasingly difficult to bear, David decided to join his brother in Arizona. His sister had passed away in 2001 and no other close relatives remained in Iowa. His fiancé, Judy, went with him and they migrated west.

After about six months, Judy decided to return to Iowa. She left David in their apartment in Arizona City, Az. He had yet to make any friends in Arizona City and found himself going crazy with loneliness. He did make friends with a woman in Phoenix via the internet and she helped a lot. When she lost her roommate in May 2007, she invited David to move in and he lived there for about a year before moving on to find a place of his own.

With a lot of time on his hands, David decided to try writing. He had never been much of a writer and had always hated writing assignments in school but he had little else to do.

There had been a story hatching in his head for years and he decided to write it. A book was born. As of this writing, he is putting the finishing touches on the fifth volume of the series while giving serious thought to the next installment.

CPSIA information can be obtained
at www.ICGtesting.com
Printed in the USA
BVHW051129060321
601818BV00011BA/1238

9 781456 311841